*Enid Blyton*

# MR STAMP-ABOUT IN A FIX

## and other stories

*Illustrated by*
*Paul Crompton*

D1327751

World International Publishing Limited
Manchester

Published in Great Britain by World International Publishing Limited,
An Egmont Company, Egmont House, PO Box 111,
Great Ducie Street,
Manchester M60 3BL.
Printed in Italy.

British Library Cataloguing in Publication Data
Blyton, Enid 1897–1968
*Mr Stamp-About in a fix and other stories.*
I. Title II. Series
823.912 [J]

ISBN 0–7498–0314–2

Cover illustration by Robin Lawrie

# Contents

# *Enid Blyton*

Enid Blyton was born in London in 1897. Her childhood was spent in Beckenham, Kent, and as a child she began to write poems, stories and plays. She trained to be a teacher but she devoted her whole life to being a children's author. Her first book was a collection of poems for children, published in 1922. In 1926 she began to write a weekly magazine for children called *Sunny Stories*, and it was here that many of her most popular stories and characters first appeared. The magazine was immensely popular and in 1953 it became *The Enid Blyton Magazine*.

She wrote more than 600 books for children and many of her most popular series are still published all over the world. Her books have been translated into over 30 languages. Enid Blyton died in 1968.

# Mr Stamp-About in a fix

"I've written three times to Mr Tiles to tell him to come and mend my roof!" said Mr Stamp-About to his sister. "And what does he say? He says he's too busy! Pah! Too busy to mend *my* roof! Just wait till I see him!"

"Please don't stamp on that rug," said his sister. "You're making the dust fly about. I think it's because you're so bad-tempered that people won't come and do things for you. Now stop stamping. If you *want* to beat the dust out of that rug, take it out, hang it over the line and beat it."

"Pah!" said Mr Stamp-About, and stalked out of the room. He put on his hat and went to find Mr Tiles. He found

him in a shed, getting together his tools to go and do a job.

Mr Stamp-About caught hold of him. "Ha! I suppose you were just about to come and mend my roof! Now don't you dare to say you weren't! You come along with me this minute!"

Little Mr Tiles looked at the big, fierce Mr Stamp-About. "Let go," he said. "If you force me to go with you like this I'll have to come – but I won't put your tiles on properly, so there!"

"Oh, yes, you will!" said Mr Stamp-About. "Because I'll sit by you and watch you! And not a penny will you get if you don't do your best work. Now bring some tiles along with you, and a pot of paint, too, to touch up the gutters. And I shall sit on a chimney-pot and watch you!"

"You will, will you?" said little Mr Tiles. "Right. I'll get the tiles – here they are. And I'll bring this pot and this brush along with me. Off we go!"

And off they went together,

Mr Stamp-About holding on fast to Mr Tiles in case he ran off. But he didn't. He walked along quite amiably, and talked about the weather.

"Fetch the ladder," said Mr Stamp-About, when they got to his house. "It's in my shed. Climb up it first and begin to put on the new tiles. I'm going to have a cup of hot cocoa as it's a cold day. Then I'll come up the ladder, and sit on a chimney-pot to watch you. I'll have a fine view of your work, I can tell you!"

Mr Tiles went to fetch the ladder. He set it up against the gutter and climbed up. Mr Stamp-About had disappeared into the house to get his cocoa. Dear, dear – he hadn't even thought of offering cold Mr Tiles a cup. Still, that suited Mr Tiles all right. He had something to do before Mr Stamp-About came out again!

He climbed the ladder quickly, taking his tiles with him. He set them down on the roof and then went back for his pot and his brush. He grinned as he brought those up. He took a quick look down. Mr Stamp-About was nowhere to be seen. He was somewhere in the house, having cocoa and biscuits!

Mr Tiles looked at the two chimneys sticking up out of the roof. One was smoking. One wasn't, so that was the one that Mr Stamp-About would sit on to watch Mr Tiles doing his work! Aha!

Mr Tiles climbed up to the chimney-pot. It was squat and round. He took his brush and dipped it into his pot. He painted the rim of the pot round and round and round.

But not with paint. Oh, no! There was no paint in that pot – there was glue. Nice, sticky glue! Aha, Mr Stamp-About, you didn't know that, did you, because the pot was labelled "White Paint"!

Mr Tiles grinned. He slid down to where the roof needed new tiles and set to work. Presently he heard Mr Stamp-About climbing up the ladder. He saw him clambering up to the chimney-pot and sitting himself flat down on it, just as if it were a stool. Mr Tiles grinned to himself.

"Now, get on, Tiles," said Stamp-About. "I can see everything you do. You're to work well and quickly. I'm not going to pay you too much, either."

"You're going to pay me twenty pounds," said Mr Tiles. "Or your sister is. Twenty pounds, Mr Stamp-About – part-payment for this work, and part-payment for your bad temper!"

If Mr Stamp-About hadn't been stuck fast to the chimney-pot he would have fallen off in rage. He stamped his feet on the roof and loosened another tile.

"That's no good!" said Mr Tiles. "That will cost you even more for another tile. Still, stamp about, Stamp-About. I don't mind you paying me more money!"

Stamp-About shouted, roared and stamped. Mr Tiles took no notice. He finished his work and went down the ladder. "Twenty one pounds!" he shouted to Stamp-About. "I'll get it from your sister as I'm sure you won't give it to me!"

Mr Stamp-About tried to get up from his chimney-pot seat, but he couldn't. Something seemed to be holding him back. What *could* it be?

"Come back! Don't you dare to ask my sister to pay you!" he yelled. "I'll pay you ten pounds and that's too much!"

"Goodbye," said Mr Tiles, jumping off the ladder. "Be careful you don't loosen any more tiles!"

He went into the house and told Stamp-About's sister she was to pay him twenty one pounds. She took it out of the cash box and gave it to him. He beamed and went out.

"Where's my brother?" called the sister. "I must just be certain the amount is right."

"He won't come in for a bit," said Mr Tiles with a grin. "You can ask him then."

Off he went, looking back now and again to see the furious Mr Stamp-About. There he sat on the chimney, trying his best to get up, but the glue was much too strong for him. He raged and stamped and shouted, and soon a collection of interested people came to watch.

"I'm stuck, I'm stuck!" he yelled. "Get me down!"

But people were afraid of his bad temper, and, besides, they were pleased to see horrid old Stamp-About stuck up on his own chimney-pot. And will you believe it, there he had to stay till a downpour of rain came and thinned out the glue.

Poor Mr Stamp-About. He was soaked through, and he missed his footing as he climbed down the roof, bounced down the ladder, and landed with a bump on the ground.

"Stamp-About! What *do* you think you are doing, sitting on a chimney-pot, shouting and yelling like that, and then falling off the roof?" cried his sister. "I'm ashamed of you. You can go straight up to bed. I've had enough of you today!"

And you'll hardly believe it, but Stamp-About had had such a lesson that he did go straight up to bed. He never forgot his day on the chimney-pot – and neither did anyone else!

## They met Mr Pinkwhistle

In Breezy Wood there was a lovely little glade, with trees that were easy to climb, and a little pond that rippled in the breeze.

One of the trees had a low branch. It was strong enough to take three children at once, and they could swing up and down, up and down, as long as they liked. All the children liked doing that, even the big ones.

Five children came down to play in the little glade every Saturday. They were all small – three girls and two boys. Joan, Kitty, Alice, John, and Eric. They sailed their boats on the shallow little pond, swung on the tree branch, and climbed the trees.

And then one day two big boys found the little glade. They looked around in delight.

"Just the place for us!" said Roy. "Trees to climb – water to paddle in – somewhere to make a camp-fire!"

"We'll find a hole in one of these trees, and make it a hiding place for our boats and sweets and balls," said Terence. "And it shall be *our* glade – nobody else's!"

So they put up a notice on one of the trees. "PRIVATE. KEEP OUT!"

When the five children got there on the next Saturday, they saw the notice. "What does it mean?" said Alice. "This place isn't private! It's for anyone!"

"I shall take the notice down," said Eric boldly. So he did. Then they began their games, swinging on the low branch and sailing boats on the pool.

Now, very soon Terence and Roy came along, carrying the things they meant to hide in the old hollow tree. They heard the shouts of the children as they came, and they were angry.

"Kids! And they've taken our notice down – look!" said Terence. "Let's chase them away."

"Well – there are five of them," said Roy, who was not very brave. "And anyway, they'll come back as soon as we've gone. We want this place for our very own."

The boys looked at one another. "Let's frighten them with some tale or other," said Roy. "We'll pretend there are some escaped bears or something hiding in this wood, in the glade, or nearby. They'll rush off soon enough then!"

"All right. Let's pretend we've been chased by bears," said Terence with a giggle. "We'll scare the silly kids properly. Come on now – yell and scream, and rush about!"

So the five small children playing happily in the glade suddenly stopped in alarm when they heard fearful yells and screams coming from the bushes not far off. They heard the sound of running feet, then more yells.

"He's nearly got me! Help! The biggest bear I ever saw!"

"Save me! Save me! There's a big snake after me!"

It was only Terence and Roy, of course, pretending to be frightened just to scare the children. They suddenly ran into the glade, yelling, and the children almost jumped out of their skins!

"Run! Run! There are some escaped animals here!" cried Roy. "Don't come back here. It's dangerous. They may have their dens in this glade. Run for your lives!"

The children ran. Kitty cried as she went, and Joan caught her foot on a root and fell over. She cried as she got up and ran again. They were all very frightened.

But after a week or two they forgot their fright, and thought that whatever escaped animals there were must surely have been caught by now.

"We'll go back to the glade," said

John. "We will go carefully, and look about. I told my mummy about the escaped bears and snakes, and she only laughed. I'm sure it's safe."

So the five children went cautiously back to the glade they liked so much. Roy and Terence were there. They were building a little fire, to roast potatoes on. Roy saw the children first, and nudged Terence.

"Here are those kids again. Climb up a tree quickly, and make some noises."

Up they went, and were well hidden by the time the five children came along.

"Someone's building a fire here – and that's not allowed," said Joan. "I'll knock it down."

She stamped on it – and that made Roy feel very angry. He sent out a fierce, deep growl. Terence did the same, and the five children stood still in sudden fright.

"What was that?" whispered Joan. "It sounded like a growl."

"Would it – would it be a bear?" asked Kitty fearfully.

Then Roy decided to hiss like a snake. "S-S-S-SSSSSSSS!"

"That was a snake!" cried Alice. "They're still here, the snakes and the bears. Quick, run!"

Such fierce growls and enormous hisses came at that moment that all five children took to their heels and fled. They ran and they ran – and at last came to the stile they had to climb over to get into the lane.

A little man was just about to get over the stile. He looked in surprise at the five panting, frightened children. Kitty was crying loudly.

"What's the matter?" said the little man. It was Mr Pinkwhistle, of course, the little fellow who is half human and half a brownie. He goes about the world putting wrong things right, as everyone knows. Dear, dear – surely there was something very wrong here!

John told him all about the two boys who had warned them of the bears and snakes – and how, when they had gone back to the glade that morning they had heard growls and hisses, and had run for their lives.

Mr Pinkwhistle guessed at once that there was some horrid trick, of course. He wiped Kitty's eyes. "Now you all go off and play somewhere else," he said. "Come back to the glade this afternoon, and you will see a notice up. It will say, 'ALL SAFE HERE', and you will know I've cleared away anything that shouldn't be there."

"Oh, thank you," said the children.

They went off together, looking back at Mr Pinkwhistle and thinking what a kind little man he was.

Now Mr Pinkwhistle, being half a brownie, could make himself invisible if he wanted to – and just at that minute he wanted to very badly. So, hey presto – he vanished, and only his shadow lay behind him, moving along as he walked towards the glade.

The two boys were there, building their fire again and giggling as they thought of the scared children.

"Didn't they run?" said Terence. "Don't you think I growled well?"

"Well, what about my hissing?" said Roy. "I'm sure no snake ever hissed louder!"

"Fancy *believing* our silly stories about bears and things," said Terence. "As if escaped animals would live in this glade!"

Pinkwhistle decided it was about time that he began his performance. Aha! He could imitate any animal under the sun – bears, lions, snakes, wolves, hyenas!

He was invisible. He could move where he liked, the two boys couldn't see him. He went to a nearby tree and shook a branch violently as if some animal was hiding there. And he grunted – grunted like a big grizzly bear.

Roy and Terence looked up at once. "What was that?"

"Something grunting – in that tree," said Roy. But by now the tree had stopped swishing about, and Pinkwhistle had gone to a small bush. He crawled underneath, making the branches move, and began roaring. You should have heard him! Why, even the lions at the zoo would have listened in astonishment.

Terence clutched Roy in great alarm. "What *is* it? Something different now. It's hiding under that bush. It sounds – oh, Roy, it sounds like a lion!"

"Let's run," said Roy. But they couldn't. They just couldn't move, they were so scared. Pinkwhistle came out from the bush and went quietly over beside the boys. They couldn't see him, of course, because he was still invisible.

He stroked their legs and hissed. What a hiss! "Sssssssssss!"

"Snakes – round our legs! Where are

they? I can't see them!" yelled Roy, and he was so frightened that he sat down suddenly. His legs wouldn't bear him any longer. Mr Pinkwhistle decided to change his stroking and hissing into galloping and neighing.

So the two boys then had to listen to feet apparently galloping round the glade, and a great neighing, as if three or four horses were there together.

"They'll gallop over us!" cried Roy – and then the galloping stopped, and a quacking began.

"Quack, quack, quack! Quack, quack, quack!"

"Ducks – but there aren't any here!" said Roy, almost crying. "Let's go, let's go! It's like a bad dream."

A howl like a dog's came right in his ear, and he leapt to his feet. He yelled – and he ran. My word, how he ran! He would have won all the running races in his school sports if he had been running in them at that moment!

Terence ran too, stumbling as he

went, looking fearfully at every bush and tree for some animal in hiding. They didn't stop running till they came to the stile. Then, panting and exhausted, they climbed to the top, and sat there, looking back over the field towards the glade.

A little man appeared beside them, and they jumped. It was Mr Pinkwhistle, of course, not invisible any longer.

"Oh! You made me jump! I didn't see you coming," said Roy.

"You seem rather alarmed about something," said Pinkwhistle, beaming at them. "What's the matter?"

"Well – we've heard bears – and lions – and horses galloping, and ducks – over in that glade," said Roy, shaking, as he thought of them.

"Dear me," said Mr Pinkwhistle. "Some small children I met this morning told me about them. They ran, too. They said two boys had warned them that there were escaped animals about.

Perhaps you were the two boys who so kindly told them?"

"Er – well – yes, we did say something about animals and snakes," said Terence. "We told the kids not to go to that glade."

"Then surely it was foolish of *you* to go there," said Pinkwhistle. "It was asking for trouble, wasn't it? I mean – if you were so certain that there were bears and snakes there, why did you go?"

Terence and Roy didn't know what to say to that. They didn't want to tell this strange little man that they had told the children a lot of untruths just to get them out of the glade and make them afraid to come back.

A cow in a field nearby suddenly mooed. Roy almost fell off the stile.

"Dear, dear – how scared you are!" said Pinkwhistle. "That was only the cow over there. Would you like to go back to that glade with me, and hunt for these animals you say are there?"

"No!" cried both boys at once, and

they leapt off the other side of the stile at once. "No, oh, no!"

"I'll never go back to that glade as long as I live!" said Roy. "Never!"

"Nor will I!" said Terence, and they both ran off at top speed as if they were afraid that Pinkwhistle would take them back with him! How he laughed to see them go.

"Now they know what it's like to be scared," he said. "Maybe they won't frighten small children again. Well – I enjoyed that, though I've made my throat a bit sore with all that roaring."

And off went little Mr Pinkwhistle down the road. One more thing put right – a very good morning's work.

That afternoon the five children went cautiously to the wood once more. The first thing they saw was a big notice.

"Hurray!" they said. "Now we can play here again. That kind little man has chased the animals away. Who *could* he have been?"

Well – *we* could tell them couldn't we?

## Miss Waddle-Toes

Once upon a time there was a little girl called Anna. She lived in a big house with a very big garden. She was a dear, pretty little girl – except when she walked! And dear me, when she walked, *how* she turned in her toes!

"I shall call you Miss Waddle-Toes," said her mother. "You walk like a duck, Anna. It looks dreadful. Do turn your feet out, not in!"

But Anna wouldn't bother to remember to turn out her toes properly. She turned them in as much as ever, and only laughed when Mummy called her Miss Waddle-Toes.

Now one day Anna had a great surprise. She found a tiny fairy caught in a spider's web, crying loudly for help. The little girl tore the web, frightened away the big spider there, and set the small fairy on the ground.

"You are very kind," said the fairy gratefully. "What can I do for you in return?"

Anna was excited.

"Please," she said, "I have always wanted to go to a fairy party. Do you think I could?"

"Yes," said the fairy at once. "There is a dance tonight under the big oak tree at the bottom of your garden. But it's fancy dress."

"Oh dear!" said Anna. "I haven't a fancy dress, I'm afraid."

"Well, come anyhow," said the fairy. "We can dress you up somehow, I expect!"

So Anna ran inside, feeling so excited that her mother really could *not* think what was the matter with her!

That night, when the moon rose high in the starry sky, Anna slipped out of bed and ran to the window. Yes – it must be time to go to the party, because she could see tiny lights gleaming here and there at the bottom of the garden. Oh, what fun!

The little girl slipped on her dressing-gown, ran downstairs, let herself quietly out of the garden door, and ran down to the bottom of the garden.

The party had begun! The garden was lit with tiny lanterns, and hundreds of pixies, elves, brownies, and gnomes were there, all in fancy dress, talking in high twittering voices, and dancing round and round with each other.

"Hello!" cried a voice, and a gnome danced up to her. "Here comes Miss Waddle-Toes, with her toes turned in as usual! Have you come to the party?"

"Yes," said Anna. "The fairy I saved from a spider today said I could come."

"Well, you must have a fancy dress," said the gnome, "and you must be made smaller, or you won't be able to dance with us. Wait till I get my wand, then

I'll give you some kind of fancy dress."

He ran off and fetched a tiny silver wand with a glittering star on the end. He looked at Anna.

"I don't know what sort of fancy dress will come when I touch you with my wand," he said. "You don't mind, do you?"

"Not at all," said Anna, hoping very much she would have a fairy's dress or perhaps a brownie's suit. "I *should* like something with wings, though."

"Right!" said the gnome. He waved his wand, said a word three times – a very magic one – and touched Anna lightly on the hair, saying, "Change, Miss Waddle-Toes, change! Wear your fancy dress till daybreak!"

Anna felt something funny happening to herself. She was certainly changing. She looked down at herself – and what a dreadful shock she got!

What do you suppose she had changed into? Why, a large yellow duckling with a pair of little flappy wings!

"Quack!" cried Anna in dismay. "Quack!"

"Goodness! She's changed into a duck!" shouted the gnome – and a lot more of the little folk came running up. "Look at that!"

"Well, she shouldn't turn her feet in!" said an elf wisely. "She might have known she'd wear a duck's dress for fancy dress, if she waddled about like one! I've often seen her turning in her toes – dreadful! Never mind, Anna! You are small enough to join us and enjoy the party now."

"Quack, quack, quack!" said poor Anna, who felt she would not enjoy the party at all! She could only quack, not talk, and she waddled along turning in her toes all the time, and couldn't dance a bit! She couldn't even fly, for her wings were really much too small. It was all most disappointing!

"How I wish I had never turned my feet in!" she thought to herself, as she tried to dance with a small fairy in butterfly's dress. "Oh dear – my feet are so big that I keep tramping on this dear little fairy's toes!" She tried to say she was sorry, but all she could say was "Quack, quack, quack!"

However, the fairy understood. "Don't mention it," she said politely, and on they danced.

The party would have been simply lovely, but Anna couldn't even eat or drink, because she didn't know how to manage her big beak! It seemed to get in the way so! In fact, it got in her way just as much as her feet did!

"This is a horrible party after all," thought the disappointed little girl. "I can't dance properly – I can't fly – I can't eat this lovely jelly – I can't drink that lovely pink lemonade – and I've never had *pink* lemonade before! I wish I'd never come!"

She sat down on the grass and watched the others dancing. It was a pretty sight – but Anna was sad. She hated being a duckling. It was horrid to waddle about in a clumsy manner when everyone else was dancing so lightly on tiptoe.

"I'll never turn my toes in again, that's certain!" thought Anna. "I didn't know how clumsy it was till I wore this duck fancy dress and was turned into a duck. I won't be so silly again."

When dawn came the fairy folk fled – and Anna was left sitting on the grass alone. She was upset. Suppose she stayed a duckling! Whatever would her mother say?

She waddled back up the garden and into the house. She walked up the stairs. She did not dare to call Mummy, because she knew she would quack. She got into bed, pulled up the clothes with two little arm-wings, and then fell asleep.

And in the morning she was herself again! Yes, really – she had her own feet and arms and everything – she was a little girl and not a duckling. How glad she was!

She jumped out of bed and dressed. Then she ran to tell Mummy her adventure, and dear me – how nicely she turned her toes out as she ran! No more Miss Waddle-Toes for her!

Mummy was sorry she had had such a horrible time at the party. "Never mind," she said, "perhaps next time it will be nicer – especially if you remember not to walk like a duck any more, Anna! Try hard and see if you can walk like a pixie does!"

Anna *is* trying hard – and if you know any little Miss Waddle-Toes just tell them what happened to Anna. They will soon stop turning in their toes, won't they?

# *Pull, Mr Stamp-About, pull!*

One day little Mr Plump went shopping with his big shopping-basket. He shouldn't have taken that basket because the bottom of it was falling to pieces, as Mrs Plump had often told him.

But he forgot, and took it along to the shops. He bought a nice currant cake at the baker's. He bought a bunch of carrots at the greengrocer's. He bought a box of chocolates at the sweet shop.

Then he went to the butcher, and got the Sunday joint. He didn't notice that the bottom was falling out of his basket. Bump! The cake fell out. Thud! Down went the carrots! Bump! That was the nice little box of chocolates.

The joint was too big to fall out. Mr Plump didn't notice his shopping dropping on to the path. He saw the joint in the basket, and thought that the other things were underneath.

But somebody else noticed the things falling out! That was Mr Stamp-About, who happened to be walking just behind Mr Plump when the cake dropped out.

He guessed what was happening at once! Aha! There was a hole in Mr Plump's basket!

Now most people would at once have run after Mr Plump and told him what was happening. But not Mr Stamp-About. Oh, no. He just picked up the cake and popped it into his own basket. Then he waited for the next thing to drop. Hurrah! Carrots! They went into his basket, too. And the box of chocolates followed them.

Little Mrs Trot saw what Mr Stamp-About was doing, and she was upset. She was afraid of Mr Stamp-About, because he had a very bad temper, but she thought she really must tell poor Mr Plump.

So she hurried up to him and whispered: "Mr Plump! You are dropping things out of your basket, and Mr Stamp-About has picked them up and put them into his!"

Mr Plump stopped and looked into his basket. There was only the joint there. He glared at Mr Stamp-About.

"Have you picked up my shopping?" he said.

"Certainly not," said Mr Stamp-About, most untruthfully.

Mr Plump looked into Mr Stamp-About's basket, and there he saw all his lost shopping. He pointed at them. "You are a thief, Mr Stamp-About. Give me them back at once, or I will fight you!"

"Rubbish! I am stronger than you," said Mr Stamp-About, scornfully.

"You're not!"

"I am! You're big and fat, but you're not strong like me," said Mr Stamp-About.

Then an idea came into Mr Plump's head. "Let's prove who is the stronger of us two! I've got a rope here, see? I'll go round this corner, and you stay here, and pull hard. If you can pull me round the corner, you can keep my shopping. If you can't, I'll have them back!"

"Right!" said Mr Stamp-About, who was quite certain he could pull Mr Plump round the corner at once. He took one end of the rope, and Mr Plump took the other and disappeared round the corner.

A crowd began to gather. "I'll tell you when to pull," said Jinky, Mr Plump's friend. He peeped round the corner at Mr Plump and grinned. He felt certain that Mr Plump was up to something!

So he was. He was busy tying his end of the rope to a lamp post. Ha! pull, Mr Stamp-About, pull all you like!

"Now – one, two, three, PULL!" yelled Jinky. And Mr Stamp-About pulled. My, how he pulled! He breathed hard, and he pulled till he turned purple.

Everyone yelled to him. "Pull, Mr Stamp-About, pull! Pull hard! Go on, Mr Stamp-About, PULL, PULL, PULL!"

And Mr Stamp-About pulled till his arms nearly came out. But although the lamp post moved about half an inch, it wouldn't move any more – and as for Mr Plump, he wasn't there at all!

No – he had run all the way round the next corner, and the next, and lo and behold! there he was round the third corner, just behind Mr Stamp-About, who was pulling for all he was worth. Behind him was his basket, full of Mr Plump's dropped shopping. Mr Plump saw it, snatched it up, and ràn off home with it, his basket of meat in the other hand. The crowd saw him, and laughed, for little Mrs Trot had told them all about it.

"Pull, Mr Stamp-About, pull!" yelled everyone. "You're not as strong as you thought you were. Pull! Pull! Pull!"

Mr Stamp-About was angry. How

dare Mr Plump pull against him so hard? He gave a jerk at the rope and the lamp post moved a little. Mr Stamp-About gave another jerk, and dear me, the lamp-post shook and shivered.

"He's coming!" said Mr Stamp-About, pleased. "Aha, Mr Plump is coming! He'll soon be round the corner at a run – and then I'll pull his nose for him!"

He gave a simply enormous tug at the rope and the lamp post came out of the ground with a crash. Mr Plod the policeman, who happened to be walking just on the opposite side of the road, was very startled to see the lamp post jump out of the ground and then crash down.

"What's all this?" he said to himself. Then he saw that a rope was tied to it. "My goodness me – somebody is actually pulling lamp posts up!"

He went round the corner at a run, and Mr Stamp-About, who had expected to see Mr Plump coming, was most astonished to see the policeman instead.

"Ah, Mr Stamp-About, so it's you, is it, pulling lamp posts up!" roared Mr Plod angrily. "How dare you? Are you mad? Tying ropes to lamp posts and yanking them up like that! You come along with me!"

"I didn't tie ropes round a lamp post!" said Mr Stamp-About, indignantly. "I tell you I didn't."

"Well, I don't care who did the rope tying. It's you that is doing the pulling," said Mr Plod.

"But – but – I wasn't pulling at a lamp post, I was pulling at Mr Plump," said Mr Stamp-About.

"Story-teller! I saw Mr Plump going into his cottage a few minutes ago with his shopping," said Mr Plod. "Do you want me to tie *you* up with that rope, Mr Stamp-About? If you don't come along with me, I will!"

"B-b-b-but – " began Mr Stamp-About again, more puzzled than ever. Mr Plod didn't want to listen to any more.

"Stop your butting, or I'll think you're

a goat," he said. "Come along! You'll have to pay for that lamp post to be mended and put back again."

"Where's my basket?" said Mr Stamp-About, looking round. "Where's my *basket*?"

Nobody said a word. But everyone grinned and Jinky let out a great big haw-haw-haw. Mr Stamp-About lost his temper. He stamped and he raged, till Mr Plod took hold of his coat collar and marched him quickly off to the police station.

As for Mr Plump, he didn't go near Mr Stamp-About for a long time – and how he laughed when Jinky told him that Mr Stamp-About had had to pay for the lamp post. It really served old Stamp-About right, didn't it?

## As bad as one another

"Hey, Jumpy, look what I've been given," shouted Feefo, rushing into his little cottage. "Two tickets for the pantomime."

"Oh, good," said Jumpy, looking up from his book. "Now, for goodness sake, Feefo, put them in a safe place. You know how careless you are!"

"All right, I'll put them into the teapot," said Feefo. "The *best* teapot, the one we never use."

So he popped them in and shut the lid. But who should come the very next day but Great Aunt Frowny, so out came the best china with its lovely teapot.

"Whatever's this in the teapot?" said Feefo when he made the tea. He fished out two pieces of wet paper.

"Feefo, those are the pantomime tickets!" shouted Jumpy. "You put them there yesterday, and now they're all wet with tea. Give them to me. I'll dry them and put them in a very, VERY safe place."

So he dried them, and then looked round for somewhere safe to put them. Ah – what about inside one of his slippers, the ones he liked to slip on at night when he toasted himself in front of the fire? His toes would feel them there when he put the slippers on, and that would remind him they were in a safe place. So into one of the slippers they went.

But Barker the dog, who loved playing with slippers, found them beside the fire, and began to toss them up in the air. Something fell out of one and he pounced on it. It was the tickets, of course.

"Now for a little chew," thought Barker, and he lay down on the rug.

"What are you chewing, Barker?" said Feefo, and went to see. He gave a yell. "Jumpy! Barker's got our pantomime

tickets! He's chewing them. Bad dog!"

"Oh dear – I put them into my slippers," said Jumpy. "I thought they'd be QUITE safe there. How was I to know that Barker would be so silly?"

"Give them to me," said Feefo, snatching them. "They're not safe with you, Jumpy, *I'll* put them somewhere *really* safe!"

"Well, who put them into the teapot and got them soaked with tea?" shouted Jumpy crossly.

Feefo ran upstairs, and put the tickets into the pocket of his pyjama jacket. At least they would be safe *there*! He wouldn't tell that silly Jumpy where he had put them, either.

Now next day Dame Soapy came to do the washing, and she took Jumpy's pyjamas and Feefo's too, and popped them into her tub of soapy water. She was most surprised to see two pulpy little bits of paper floating about in the suds. She picked them out and called to Jumpy.

"Hey, Mr Jumpy, see what's in my suds. It must have been something in the pocket of the pyjamas I'm washing."

Jumpy took them. "Oh, that Feefo!" he shouted. "He must have put the tickets into his pyjama pocket. Feefo, Feefo! Come here, you silly, stupid fellow!"

Feefo came running and Jumpy showed him the tickets, all wet and soft. "See these – they've been in the soapy water! Did you put them in your pyjama pocket?"

"Yes, I did. And it would have been a very, very safe place if Dame Soapy hadn't taken them to wash!" said Feefo.

"Well, I never – so you're blaming *me*, are you?" said Dame Soapy in a temper. "All right, I'll leave you to do your washing yourself, Mr Feefo, pockets and tickets and all!"

And away she went, wiping her soapy hands on her apron. Feefo and Jumpy stared at one another in dismay.

"There now, she's gone – and we'll

have to do all that washing ourselves!" said Jumpy. "Well, you shan't have the tickets again, Feefo, I promise you that! I'll dry them and put them in a safe place myself – a REALLY safe place this time!"

"Well, you'd better tell me where, or you may forget," said Feefo, snappily. "You know what your memory's like – it's just a forgettery!"

Jumpy was angry. He went upstairs for a while and then came down.

"Well – I've put them in a very, very safe place – so safe that nothing can possibly happen to them before we go to the pantomime," he said.

Well, the pantomime day came at last. Feefo and Jumpy felt excited. They did love a pantomime! They both changed into their very best clothes, and then they each brushed the other down, and put on their hats.

Off they went, talking happily about what they would see at the pantomime.

They arrived at the theatre, and went

in at the big front doors.

"Tickets, please," said a man.

Feefo turned to Jumpy. "Tickets," he said. "You've got them, haven't you?"

"Er – no – goodness me, I've forgotten them," said Jumpy. "Oh my, I'll have to go back and get them! Where did I put them? Feefo, where did I put them?"

"You didn't tell me," said Feefo. "Oh, you silly fellow! You turnip-head! Come back quickly or we shall miss half the show."

So they hurried back to look for the tickets – but it was no good, poor Jumpy could *not* remember where he had put them! In this drawer or that? No! On that shelf? No! In that jug? No!

"Oh, don't let's hunt any more. Let's go back to the pantomime," said Feefo at last. "And you can *pay* for the tickets, Jumpy. It will serve you right. We shall miss half of it as it is."

So back they went, and Jumpy put his hand into his trouser pocket to pay for the tickets. He drew out his money –

and something else! He stared into his hand in surprise, and then gave such a yell that Feefo leapt into the air in fright.

"I've got the tickets! Here in the pocket of my best trousers! I put them there, because I knew I'd be wearing them today, and so I'd *have* to take the tickets with me. And I *did* take them – they're here, look!"

"Jumpy, I really do think you are just about the silliest fellow I've ever known," said Feefo. "And why I chose you to be my friend I can't imagine. We ran all the way home – and you had those tickets in your trouser pocket all the time!"

"*And* you've missed half the show," said the man at the ticket office, grinning. "Hadn't you better go in before you miss the other half?"

So in they went, still squabbling – and which of them is going to keep things safely next time, I really don't know. They're both as bad as one another!

## *Mister Do-As-I-Like*

Everyone called him Do-As-I-Like, because he always said "I do as I like" – and, what is more, he did! He was a vain little bully of a goblin, bad-tempered and tiresome. How everyone hated Do-As-I-Like!

One day he met little Mr Smarty. Mr Smarty was a goblin too, and today he was dressed in his best.

"Oho!" said Mr Do-As-I-Like, standing in front of him. "You're looking very, very smart today, Mr Smarty. I hear you've got a shop. What about taking me there and dressing me from top to toe? I could do with a new suit and hat."

"Er – well – I'm in a bit of a

hurry today, Mr Do-As-I-Like," said Mr Smarty, trying to edge away.

"Are you? Well, so am I," said Do-As-I-Like. "Come on, let's hurry along to your shop, Smarty. I'm going to a party tomorrow, and I want to look nice. I'll have a top hat, and a red suit, and a pair of red shoes, and . . ."

"But – but – you won't find . . ." began poor Smarty.

Do-As-I-Like stopped him. "Now, no excuses! Take me straight along to your shop. Do you want me to turn you into a worm?"

"Oh, no, no!" cried poor Smarty. "Come with me. You shall have a wonderful new set of clothes, just for the taking, Mr Do-As-I-Like!"

"Aha, that sounds more like it," said Do-As-I-Like, and he followed Smarty at once.

They came to a big street. On the corner was an enormous shop, whose windows were filled with lovely clothes. Do-As-I-Like was most impressed.

"Wonderful!" he said. "Beautiful shop you've got, Smarty. Come along in."

"You go first," said Smarty, politely. He opened the door for him. He bowed him into the shop and pointed up the stairs.

"Up there," he said. "Help yourself to anything you want. Don't bother to be polite to anyone. Just take what you like and do what you like."

"I shall," said Do-As-I-Like grandly, and he walked up the stairs. He came to another part of the shop where all kinds of clothes were set out. Do-As-I-Like saw a fine red suit. He pulled it down at once and began to try it on. It fitted him well.

An assistant came up. "Can I help you, sir?" he said.

"Yes. Get me three more suits like this, one in blue, one in yellow and one in green," said Do-As-I-Like, haughtily. "And look sharp about it. And get me top hats to match and shoes as well. I don't care about the price."

Of course he didn't. He meant Smarty to pay for all that! Soon he had a great array of clothes, and he ordered the assistant to pack them all up for him to take away.

"That will be one hundred pounds, and sixty pence sir," said the assistant, handing him an enormous parcel.

"Mr Smarty will pay," said Do-As-I-Like.

"Who's he?" said the assistant, puzzled.

"Well, he owns this shop, silly," said Mr Do-As-I-Like.

"But this is Mr Bom-Bom's Stores," said the assistant, looking even more puzzled. "I'll call him."

Bom-Bom came. He was a tall, burly gnome, with very sharp eyes indeed. "What's all this?" he said. "This is *my* shop, it doesn't belong to anyone called Smarty. You will please pay the bill or I shall call Mr Plod, the policeman."

"B-b-b-but – Mr Smarty himself brought me here!" stammered Do-As-

I-Like in amazement. "He opened the door for me, told me to go upstairs and choose what I liked."

"The only Smarty I know is Mr Smarty who owns the fish shop," said Bom-Bom, looking very fierce. "He has shut up his shop today, and dressed himself in his best to go to his niece's wedding. And what is *your* name?"

"Mr Do-As-I-Like," said the goblin in a very small voice.

"*Hmmm*! I thought so," said Bom-Bom. "Well, what about my bill? Or shall we call in Mr Plod the policeman and ask him to settle the little matter for us?"

So Do-As-I-Like had to pay, and he only had twenty pence left. "All these fine clothes, and not enough money left to buy a few sausages for my supper," he groaned. "Wait till I meet that Mr Smarty again. Just wait!"

But when he passed by Mr Smarty's fish shop the next day, and saw the little fishmonger grinning to himself, he decided not to say a word to him at all.

No – if Smarty could play a trick like that one, he might quite well think up another. It served Do-As-I-Like right, didn't it?

## Mrs Doodle loses her head

Mrs Doodle was a funny sort of person. If anything happened to upset her in any way, she made such a fuss.

When her clothes-line blew down and her washing fell into the mud, how she flapped and fussed!

"Oh, look at that! Oh my, oh my, whatever am I to do? My beautiful washing! What shall I do-oo-ooo?"

"Now don't lose your head," said Mrs Twinks, her next-door neighbour. "Really, I never knew anyone like you, Mrs Doodle, for getting into a flap about nothing!"

"Nothing!" said Mrs Doodle, indignantly, getting redder and redder in the face. "What do you mean — *nothing*? Do you call my clean washing in the mud nothing? Do you call my broken clothes-line nothing? I'd like to know what you would call something!"

It was always like that with Mrs Doodle. She made such a fuss, and got into such a state about things that it was very difficult to calm her down. Her neighbours really got very tired of it.

"She loses her head about everything," said Mrs Twinks to Mrs Gobo. "She really does."

"One day she'll lose it altogether," said Mrs Gobo, with a laugh.

One morning Mrs Doodle put a lot of paper on the fire to burn. It flared up at once, and sent big flames all the way up the chimney. Mrs Doodle hadn't had her chimney swept when she should, and it was full of soot.

The soot caught fire — and at once the flames and smoke swept right up the chimney to the very top! Smoke poured out, black and thick.

Mrs Gobo came banging at Mrs Doodle's door. "Hey! Your chimney is on fire! Hey!"

Mrs Doodle began to pant with worry. She rushed here and she rushed there. She fell over the cat. She cried and wept. But she didn't put out the fire.

"Now don't lose your head," said Mrs Gobo. "Just put some water on the fire and put out the flames. You ought to have had that chimney swept ages ago."

"Oh dear, oh my, oh my, oh dear!" groaned Mrs Doodle, and threw a whole bucketful of water towards the flames in the grate. Unluckily, she didn't throw far enough and soaked the poor cat from head to foot. It jumped in fright and scratched Mrs Doodle by accident as it ran past. She screamed, and ran round and round the kitchen, shouting out to Mrs Gobo!

"Help me, help me! The cat has scratched me, my chimney's on fire, and I don't know what to do."

"Well, you're losing your head as usual," said Mrs Gobo. She put out the fire and then dried the poor frightened cat.

"I don't lose my head," said Mrs Doodle, crossly. "Don't say that. It's a stupid thing to say. I never lose my head about things. I am very sensible."

Mrs Gobo laughed. "Well, well! If that is what you call being sensible, I don't know how you behave when you're silly!"

Mrs Gobo went out. On the way home she met Dame Tip-Tap, who knew a lot of magic. Mrs Gobo told Dame Tip-Tap all about Mrs Doodle.

"She's such a fusser," she said. "I wish we could cure her. She is always losing her head about things."

"Well," said Dame Tip-Tap, with a twinkle in her eye, "I know some magic that makes people's heads disappear. Shall we try it on Mrs Doodle? You understand – her head doesn't *really* go – it's just that we can't see it. It's still there, but can't be seen. Perhaps if I use my magic and make her lose her head like that, it will teach her not to make such a fuss about things."

"Oooh – that would be funny," said Mrs Gobo, with a chuckle. So, the very next time that Mrs Doodle began to squeal and cry and make a fuss, Mrs Gobo hurried along to her house with Dame Tip-Tap.

Dame Tip-Tap flicked a little yellow powder over Mrs Doodle's head when she wasn't looking and muttered some very magic words under her breath. Mrs Doodle was in a great state because her cat had stolen some sausages, and she was chasing the animal round the kitchen with a broom. She had been just about to go out, and had put her hat on her head – a pretty, flowery hat with ribbons.

Just as Dame Tip-Tap finished whispering the magic words, Mrs Doodle's head vanished. It simply wasn't there any more. At least, nobody could see it! Mrs Gobo stared in wonder and amazement. There was Mrs Doodle, quite all right up to her neck. Then there was a space – and then her flowery hat. No head at all.

"What are you staring at, Mrs Gobo?" said Mrs Doodle's voice, most annoyed. "Isn't my hat straight on my head?"

"I don't know," said Mrs Gobo. "You've lost your head! Your hat is there all right – but your head is gone!"

"Stuff and nonsense!" said Mrs Doodle, very sharply indeed. She went to the mirror and gazed into it. But she couldn't see her head, because it had vanished. But there was her flowery hat, neatly perched in the air, going wherever Mrs Doodle went. It was most peculiar.

"Oh, oh, oh!" squealed Mrs Doodle, in a dreadful fright. "Where's my head? Where's it gone?"

"I said you'd lose it one day," said Mrs Gobo, beginning to laugh. "You always lost it over the silliest little

things – and now it really has gone. You shouldn't make such a fuss, Mrs Doodle – then you would keep your head and be sensible, like me and Mrs Twinks."

"I'm going to the doctor," said poor Mrs Doodle, in a greater fright than ever. "I'm going to the doctor."

She rushed out into the street. How people stared to see her coming along without any head at all! Her hat bobbed along perkily, but it didn't seem to be sitting on any head. It was most comical. Everyone laughed loudly. They felt certain that Dame Tip-Tap had used some of her magic, and they enjoyed the joke.

The doctor rubbed his eyes when Mrs Doodle burst into his house. "Who are you?" he said. "Haven't you forgotten something? You seem to have left your head at home."

"Doctor, Doctor, make me better!" begged Mrs Doodle. "Where's my head? It's gone! I know I do lose my head and get into dreadful fusses when things don't happen as I want them to – but, oh, I never never thought my head would vanish like this. Give me some medicine to get it back."

"I can't," said the doctor, watching the flowery hat nodding up and down. "You'll have to go without your head till it comes back of its own accord, Mrs Doodle. Then be careful never to lose it again!"

Mrs Doodle hurried back home, very frightened and miserable. She didn't see Dame Tip-Tap behind her, blowing some purple powder over her hat, whispering magic words all the while. Her head appeared again at once, but she didn't know it. Everyone saw it come back, and most people were rather glad. It was all right to lose your head for a little while, but not for always!

Mrs Doodle went into her bedroom to take off her hat, and goodness, gracious me, there was her head back again under the hat, the eyes staring at her, and tears trickling down the cheeks.

"Oh! I've got my head back!" cried Mrs Doodle in delight. "Mrs Gobo! Mrs Gobo! Mrs Twinks! Dame Tip-Tap! My head's back. It feels fine. It's as firm as can be. I only lost it for a little while. Does it look all right?"

"Quite all right," said Mrs Gobo, coming into the bedroom. "But, Mrs Doodle, yours must be a strange kind of head, if you can lose it as easily as that. It's come back this time all right, but it might not another time. So do be careful, won't you?"

"Oh, yes, I will!" said Mrs Doodle, wiping the tears away. "Oh, I do feel so happy now. Come and have a cup of tea with me, all of you. Do!"

So they did. Mrs Doodle boiled the kettle, and when she went to make the tea she burnt herself on the hot kettle.

"Oh!" she yelled, and danced round the kitchen, squealing. "Oh! You horrid kettle! Why did you do that?"

Everyone watched Mrs Doodle's head as if they expected it to vanish again.

Mrs Doodle remembered, and rushed to the glass to see if it was still there. It was.

"I must be careful," she said, calming down. "I must be very, very careful."

She is. She hardly ever gets into a fuss now. I wish I'd been there when she lost her head. Don't you?

## The clever servant

Once upon a time Lord Brainy wanted a servant. He wanted somebody clever, for he hated to have stupid people round him.

"I will put a notice in the paper," said Lord Brainy. "Then perhaps I shall get somebody clever." So he wrote a notice and put it into the village paper. This is what he said:

Wanted by Lord Brainy, a really clever servant. Call tomorrow at six o'clock.

Well, a great many people saw that notice, and wished they could get the job, for Lord Brainy was good and kind.

74

Little Wily the Pixie saw it too, and made up his mind that *he* would get the job! But how could he prove to Lord Brainy that he was clever?

"I'm so small," sighed Wily. "And I don't look at all clever. But I am – I know I am. I would be just the right person for Lord Brainy!"

He sat and thought for a long time. His dog crept up to him and put his nose on Wily's knee. His cat rubbed against

his leg, purring – but for once Wily took no notice of them.

At last he jumped up and rubbed his hands. He had thought of an idea! How he hoped that it would work!

He took his watch from his pocket and went to the larder with it. He put it beside the joint of meat! How strange! But Wily knew what he was doing. Then he took off his tie and folded it carefully beside the packet of kippers on the larder shelf.

His dog and cat sniffed in delight at the meat and the kippers. But Wily did not give them any. He shut the larder door tightly, and went back into the kitchen. He took his best suit and sponged and pressed it. He meant to look his very smartest when he went to see Lord Brainy the next day.

At six o'clock the next evening Wily went to Lord Brainy's big house. He took with him his faithful dog and cat. Wagger the dog walked close beside him. Purrer the cat sat on his shoulder, purring into his ear. In his pocket was his watch, and round his neck was the tie that he had put in the larder the day before!

He came to Lord Brainy's house. Lord Brainy was just coming into the garden to see if anyone was going to ask for the job of servant. There were already four people waiting.

"Good evening," said Lord Brainy. "Who came first?"

One by one the four people were seen and talked to by Lord Brainy, and told that he would let them know the next day who he had chosen. Then came Wily's turn. He looked very small, not very clever, but very clean and neat.

"You won't do, I'm afraid," said Lord Brainy. "You are so small, and you don't look very clever."

"Please, sir, I am far cleverer than I look," said Wily at once. "You really wouldn't believe the things I can do!"

Lord Brainy smiled. "Well, tell me some," he said.

"Well, sir, if you hide my watch in the middle of a great big field, and don't tell me where it is, I can find it just by walking over the field!" said Wily. "You can bury it as deep as you like — I'll know when I walk over it."

Lord Brainy laughed. "I'm afraid I don't believe that," he said. "But we'll try. Give me your watch."

So Wily gave it to him. Lord Brainy didn't know that it smelt of the meat that it had been beside all night long! He took it, locked Wily into a room, and went to bury the watch in the great field at the end of his garden.

Presently he came back, smiling. "Well, come along," he said. "It's buried somewhere in the field. Now see if you can find it just by walking over it."

Wily went out to the field. Wagger went with him, and Purrer was still on his shoulder. Wily began to walk over the field with Wagger. Up and down he went, whilst Lord Brainy watched him.

"You'll never find your watch just by

doing that!" he laughed. "It's a good thing *I* know where it is, or your watch would be lost!"

Just then Wagger began to sniff. He smelt meat with his sharp doggy nose! Where was it? He looked all round but couldn't see it. It must be in the ground then – but as soon as Wily saw Wagger getting excited he knew what the reason was! Wagger could smell meat – so his watch, which smelt of meat, must be just there!

"I think my watch is here!" Wily called to Lord Brainy. "I will dig and see!" Wily had a spade, so he began to dig – and at once he found his watch. He took it out of the earth and held it up to Lord Brainy.

"Well, well, well!" said Lord Brainy in great astonishment. "That's the cleverest thing I ever saw!"

"Oh, I can do cleverer things than that!" said Wily. "Look, sir – here is my tie. Go to that wood over there, and tie it to the branch of any tree you like.

I will walk through the wood, without looking up – and when I come to the tree where you have put it, I shall stop at once!"

"Impossible!" said Lord Brainy. "I don't think *anyone* could do that!" He took the tie and went to the wood. He chose a thick poplar tree and hid the tie there, just in *case* Wily should look up and see it.

"Now go and find it!" he said to Wily. Wily went off with Lord Brainy, and began to walk slowly through the wood. Purrer was sitting quietly on his shoulder – but suddenly the cat lifted her head and sniffed in surprise.

Kippers! She smelt kippers! But how could kippers be in a wood? Purrer knew many woods, but she had never found kippers in any of them. She felt quite excited, and sniffed hungrily.

Wily felt her getting restless, and he stopped at once. He was sure that Purrer could smell the kippery smell of his tie – and that meant that it must be

in the tree above. He looked up and saw a thick poplar tree.

"I think my tie is here," he said to Lord Brainy. He parted the branches, and sure enough, there was his tie! He pulled it down and put it round his neck.

"Well, you certainly are the most remarkably clever pixie I've ever seen," said Lord Brainy in astonishment. "I will certainly take you on as my servant."

Now Wily was a very truthful pixie, and he felt a little bit uncomfortable about his tricks, now that he had got the job and had found that Lord Brainy was so nice. He went very red and spoke humbly to his new master.

"Please, sir, I have something to say first. I am telling you the truth when I say I am clever – but I am not quite so clever as you think I am!"

"What do you mean?" asked Lord Brainy in surprise.

And then Wily told him how his dog had smelt the meat-smell of his buried watch, and how his cat had smelt the kippery tie! "You see, they were the clever ones really!" he said.

"Dear me!" said Lord Brainy in surprise. "So that explains how you found your watch and your tie in such a remarkable way! Well, you quite deceived me, Wily."

"I suppose you won't want me to be your servant now," said Wily dolefully.

"I want you all the more!" said Lord Brainy, with a laugh. "Your pets may be clever – but *you* had to think of the idea! And also, you are something that is even better than being clever – you are truthful! Yes, you shall certainly have the job, Wily, and you can come to me tomorrow!"

So off skipped Wily, as happy as a blackbird in spring – and now he is working happily for Lord Brainy. Wagger is there too, guarding the house, and Purrer catches all the mice. They are both paid sixpence a week, which they spend on bones and kippers!

## Mr Stamp-About and
## Bellow the brownie

"**H**ere comes Bellow the brownie!" said Tippy to Winks. "Let's eat our apples quickly or he'll take them from us!"

Bellow saw them gobbling their apples and he yelled at them. "Hey! Where did you get those apples?"

"Off a tree at home!" said Tippy.

Bellow caught him by the shoulder. "Have you got any more apples on you?" he said. "Turn out your pockets. Ha – empty! Well, lead me to this tree and I'll help myself."

"No, please don't. You'd take so many," said Winks. "Let Tippy go."

Bellow caught hold of Winks, too, and he shook them both very roughly.

"Lead me to this tree!" he said, in his loud voice. "Now then – quick march, both of you!"

"This way," said Tippy meekly, and walked off to the left, with Bellow still holding him fast. Winks looked at Tippy, surprised to think that he was going to lead Bellow to their precious apple tree. Tippy winked at him, which surprised Winks even more.

Down the street they went, and up the hill. Down the hill and over a field. Bellow shouted in their ears. "Go quicker! I want those apples!"

So Winks and Tippy began to trot. Tippy panted loudly, and Bellow grinned. He liked catching people and making them run!

"Where's this apple tree?" he shouted. "We ought to be nearly there."

"Not far away now," panted Tippy, and he pointed to a little house on a hill. "Soon be there!"

Winks looked at him in surprise. What was Tippy up to? That wasn't their house! It belonged to Mr Stamp-About!

They came to the gate. Bellow let go of their arms and Tippy sank down on the wall, pretending to pant heavily.

"Where's this tree?" demanded Bellow, looking into the front garden. "I can't see it."

"Go round the back," panted Tippy. "I'm so out of breath I can't walk a step farther. If there are no apples on the ground, climb the tree!"

Bellow went round to the back of the little house. Ah – there was the apple tree – but only one or two apples lay on the ground. He would climb it and stuff his pockets full.

Up the tree he went. What lovely apples! He would pick as many as he pleased – and he'd come back tomorrow and the next day, too, if he wanted to.

Tippy tiptoed round the house and

looked to see what Bellow was doing. Good – he was up the tree! He went back and whispered to Winks, and they both tiptoed up the garden path to the front door. They knocked quietly.

The door was flung open and Mr Stamp-About stood there, frowning and glaring. "What do you want to come and disturb me for in the middle of my afternoon nap?" he shouted.

"Please, Mr Stamp-About, there's somebody up your apple tree," said Tippy.

Mr Stamp-About gave a roar just like one of Bellow's and rushed round the house at once, almost knocking Tippy and Winks over. They followed him to the corner of the house and peeped around it.

Mr Stamp-About was thunderstruck to see Bellow up his apple tree, picking apples and stuffing them into his pockets! He gave such a yell that Bellow almost fell out of the tree in fright.

"HEY! YOU UP THERE! What do

you think you're DOING?" yelled Stamp-About.

Bellow was astonished to see a very angry man stamping about below the tree, glaring up at him.

"Who are you?" he said.

"What's that matter? You're up my tree, stealing my apples! What's *your* name?" shouted Stamp-About.

"This isn't your tree. It belongs to Tippy and Winks," said Bellow, scared.

"Ho, it does, does it? Then how was it that Tippy and Winks came to tell me there was a thief up my apple tree?" roared Stamp-About. "You come on down! You let me show you what happens to thieves in my apple tree!"

Bellow didn't want to come down. He felt much safer up the tree, and he really couldn't understand this at all. Tippy and Winks had certainly brought him here – so how could it be Mr Stamp-About's tree?

"I'm not coming down," he said.

"Then I'll up after you and *throw* you

down!" said Stamp-About, reaching for a low branch.

"No, no! I'll come down, I'll come down!" bellowed poor Bellow, hoping that he could jump from the lowest bough and run.

But Stamp-About was waiting for him – and what a time Bellow had! Stamp-About chased him all over the garden.

Tippy and Winks laughed and laughed. Stamp-About caught Bellow and made him empty his pockets. Then he gave him a good shake and poor Bellow went racing up the lane, bellowing at the top of his voice.

Stamp-About felt pleased with himself. He saw Tippy and Winks peeping round the corner of the house.

"Hey, you," he said. "Thanks for telling me about that rascal. You can help yourself to all the apples I made him turn out of his pockets!"

"Oh, thank you, Mr Stamp-About," said Tippy. "We've a tree at home but it's only got a few apples on it. We shall be very glad of these!"

Off they went, their pockets full. They nibbled an apple each, feeling very pleased. "You were clever, Tippy," said Winks. "Very clever indeed."

"Look – there's Bellow!" said Tippy, suddenly. "Shall we run away?"

"No. He won't want to take *these* apples!" said Winks. "He'll be afraid."

Winks was right. Bellow slunk by them like a dog with his tail down. He wasn't going to try any funny tricks with Tippy and Winks again! Why, they might lead him to a *giant* another time – poor Bellow!

## Poor Mister Booh

Mister Booh was a fat little man who lived in Chubby Cottages, down Lemon Lane. He was fat because he lived on lots of butter, eggs, cream, and milk, and he liked being fat. He said it made him feel good-tempered.

Now one day he went to a meeting to decide whether or not Lemon Lane should be widened. There was a very narrow place in the middle of it and carts couldn't pass each other there, but were always getting stuck. So Mister Booh and all the other folk living in Lemon Lane went to talk about it and to see what should be done.

Mister Booh put on his new rubber boots, because it was raining. He took his brown gloves too, because his hands got cold very easily. Then he went off to the meeting.

Everybody talked a great deal and they all enjoyed themselves very much

and felt very grand. Nothing was decided, but they said they would meet again the very next week and have another talk. Then they all went out into the hall to put on their outdoor things to go home.

Mister Booh put on his rubber boots, and took his brown gloves from the hall stand. Then he said goodbye to everyone and started off for home.

He put on his gloves as he went, and they somehow seemed rather big. His boots flip-flapped as he went too, and this surprised Mister Booh very much. He looked down at them and saw that they really hardly fitted his feet.

"Well, that's funny," he said. "Have my feet gone smaller? They fitted me well enough when I bought them last week."

Then he looked at his gloves and was more surprised than ever.

"They seem too big too," he said. "Oh dear, I'm getting thin! I wonder why that is? I must be ill. Yes, that's it, I'm going to be ill, and that's why my hands and feet are thinner and my shoes and gloves too big."

He was very much worried, and decided to call at the doctor's and tell him. So when he came to Doctor Come-in's brass plate, he went in and knocked at the door.

Doctor Come-in was at home.

"What's the matter with you?" he asked Mister Booh. "You look worried."

"Yes, Doctor, and I *feel* worried," said poor Mister Booh. "I've got much thinner in a week."

"Dear me, you look as fat as ever to me," said Doctor Come-in.

"Well, I'm not," said Mister Booh, and he showed the doctor how very much too big his boots and his gloves were. "That will show you how much thinner I've got in a week, because when I bought these new last week they fitted me very well indeed."

"Dear, dear, you must be wasting away," said Doctor Come-in. "Well, never mind – we'll soon put you right. You must eat plenty of cream, butter, and eggs, and drink lots of milk. Then you'll soon be as fat as ever again."

"Well, I eat all those now," said Mister Booh.

"Eat twice as much then," said the doctor, "and come and see me again in a week's time."

Mister Booh went home, still very much worried. He ordered twice as many eggs and twice as much butter, cream, and milk as usual. His milkman was so pleased. Mister Booh stayed indoors all that week, because he wanted to give himself a chance to get fat again.

And do you know, when the day came for him to go to the next meeting about the widening of the narrow place in Lemon Lane, he could only just get his rubber boots on! And he split the gloves – so that shows you how much bigger his hands had grown!

He was delighted. He walked to the

meeting, took off his rubber boots and gloves and went into the dining-room, where everybody was talking nineteen to the dozen.

After the meeting was over, and still nothing was decided at all, they went out into the hall again to get their things. Mister Booh found his boots, but dear, dear me, what was his surprise to find that he couldn't *possibly* get them on! They were about two sizes too small. And as for his gloves, well, he couldn't even get his thumb into the thumb-hole!

"But I can't have grown so much fatter just in the meeting," he cried, quite frightened. Everybody crowded round him to see what was the matter, and he told them.

"Oh, please," said a small voice, "I think I can explain."

Mister Booh turned round and saw a very tall, thin man with large feet and hands. He was wearing rubber boots and gloves that had split down the side.

"Well, please explain then," said

Mister Booh impatiently.

"You see, last week someone went off with my new rubber boots," said the tall man in a meek voice, "and my gloves too. He left me his small boots and gloves instead, and I had a dreadful time getting home in the boots. I didn't know whose they were, but I thought perhaps they would be brought back to this meeting, and they were. I've got them on now. Those that you have now are *really* yours, Mister Booh, and I can't think why you can't get them on."

"But I know why," groaned poor Mister Booh. "Oh dear, oh dear. I didn't guess I had on gloves and boots belonging to a bigger person than me. I thought they were my own, and I was very much worried because I felt sure my feet and hands had gone thin. So I went to the doctor and he told me how to get fatter – and now that I have my own boots and gloves back again I'm too fat to get them on."

"Poor Mister Booh," said everyone. "Whatever will you do?"

Well, of course he couldn't do anything except walk home in his stockinged feet and carry his gloves instead of wearing them. And he was very much afraid that he wouldn't be able to wear his other shoes either, or any of his gloves, and even his new suit was too tight for him.

He went past the doctor's house very quickly, because he knew that Doctor Come-in would be expecting him that day, and he didn't want to go in and explain that he really hadn't been getting thinner after all, and was now much too fat. No, the doctor would laugh if he knew that.

So he went sadly home, making no noise at all in his stockinged feet, wishing and wishing that he hadn't eaten so much butter, cream, and eggs, and thinking of all the new clothes he would have to buy.

Poor Mister Booh!

## Dame Thimble's work

Dame Thimble lived in a little house at the end of Chuckle Village. She was very clever with her needle, and could make the loveliest, frilliest dresses for the little folk that you could imagine.

They all went to her for their party dresses. She used gossamer thread for her cotton, so her stitches could never be seen. She sat in the sun and she stitched and sewed, and sewed and stitched all day long.

One day a pixie was rude to her. "Oho!" thought Dame Thimble, "next time you come to me for a frilly party dress, my dear, I'll sew a nasty little spell inside it, that I will. And you'll get

SUCH a surprise when you wear it!"

So, when the pixie came along and gave an order for a new frilly dress, Dame Thimble sewed away at it busily. She stitched a nasty little spell in it, too.

"This will make the pixie stamp and shout and put out her tongue and behave as rudely as can be!" chuckled the old dame to herself. "Then everyone will be shocked and she will be turned out of the party!"

101

She sent the frilly dress to the pixie.
But the pixie didn't want it for herself.
Oh no – it was to be a birthday present
for her cousin, the little Princess Sylfai!
She was to wear it on her birthday.

So, when her birthday came, the
Princess Sylfai put on her new frilly
dress. Her maid did it up – and then
the trouble began!

Sylfai stamped and shouted! She put
out her tongue at everyone, and she
pinched and punched anyone who came
near. The Queen, the King and the
maid were upset and distressed.

"She's ill, the poor darling," said the
Queen. "She has never behaved like this
before. Take off her new dress and pop
her into bed, please, Maid."

But, of course, as soon as the dress
was off the Princess behaved like her
own sweet self again. The Queen stared
at the frilly dress. She picked it up and
smelt it.

"There's a nasty spell sewn into it!"
she cried. "Oh, what a wicked thing to

do! Who made this dress?"

"Dame Thimble," said the maid. "Dear, dear, whatever made her do that!"

"Tell her to pack her things and leave Chuckle Village at once," said the Queen. "I won't have her using bad spells like this. My poor little Sylfai – no wonder she behaved so strangely!"

Dame Thimble was full of horror when she heard what had happened. She didn't make any excuses. She packed her things, took her work basket in her arms and left Fairyland by the first bus.

Where did she go to? Well, I've seen some of her handiwork this very day! Yes, some of the lovely delicate frills she makes so well. Shall I tell you where I saw them?

I picked some mushrooms in a field – and under their caps were scores of beautiful frills, with not a stitch in them to be seen. You don't believe me? Well, you look for them yourself then!

## *Look out for the snowman*

Mother Tuppeny was puzzled. She had twelve hens and, quite suddenly, they had almost stopped laying eggs for her.

"They have been laying so well," she said to Mr Peeko next door. "And now they hardly lay at all. What do you think is the matter with them? Shall I give them some medicine, or scold them, or what?"

"No, no," said Mr Peeko. "Your hens look healthy enough, Mother Tuppeny. Perhaps your children have been running in and out, taking the eggs?"

"Oh, no. They always bring them to me when they find any in the nests," said Mother Tuppeny. "It's a great loss,

Mr Peeko – I use such a lot of eggs for the children, you know. I don't know what to give them for breakfast now."

"Now you listen to me, Mother Tuppeny," said Mr Peeko, thinking hard. "I believe a thief may be coming in the night and stealing your eggs. You leave two eggs in one of the nests, and see if they are there the next morning."

105

So Mother Tuppeny left two eggs in the nest and looked for them the next morning. They were gone! What a shame! She ran crying to Mr Peeko.

"Those two eggs have gone – and there are none at all in the boxes. It's a thief who comes, Mr Peeko. What shall I do?"

"You go to Mr Plod, the policeman, and tell him all about it," said Mr Peeko. "He'll know what to do!"

So Mother Tuppeny went to Mr Plod. He listened gravely, then took out his big black notebook. "Now you listen carefully to me and do exactly as I tell you, Mother Tuppeny," he said. "You go home and tell your children to make a nice big snowman near your hen house, and to leave it there tonight. And if you see me come into your garden when the moon is up, don't take any notice."

So Mother Tuppeny told her children to go and make a fine snowman in her garden by the hen house, and they rushed out in delight.

Soon a great big snowman was built there, with a big round head, a long white body, stones for eyes and buttons, and a twig for his mouth. Mother Tuppeny gave the children one of her old hats and an old shawl to dress him in.

"It's a snow-woman now, not a snowman," cried the children. "Oh, look, Mother, isn't she lovely?"

"Yes, lovely," said Mother Tuppeny, laughing at the funny sight of the old snow-woman with her hat and shawl on. "Now come along in and have tea. It will soon be dark."

They left the snow-woman in the garden and went in to tea. When it got dark Mother Tuppeny thought she heard footsteps in the garden and she guessed it was Mr Plod.

It was. He went down to the hen house and found the snow-woman. He flashed his torch on her and smiled. What a funny-looking creature!

Mr Plod knocked the old snow-woman down so that there was nothing left of her. Then he stood himself in her place, with a white coat over his uniform. He put the old hat on his head, and dragged the red shawl round him. Then he stood quite still.

When the children lifted the curtain and peered out into the moonlight before they went to bed, they laughed.

"Look! There's our old snow-woman out there all alone! How funny she looks!"

"She looks taller than when we built her," said one of the boys.

"But how could she be?" said the other children. "Snow-women don't grow!"

But, of course, theirs *had* grown, because Mr Plod was quite a bit taller than the snow-woman they had built. He stood there very patiently, waiting and waiting.

Nobody came for a long, long time. Then from over the wall at the bottom came a little knobbly figure. Mr Plod tried to see who it was.

"Well, well – it's that nasty mean little Knobbly Goblin!" said Mr Plod to himself. "I've often thought he was up to mischief – and so he is!"

The Knobbly Goblin crept to the hen house. He suddenly saw the snowman – or what he thought was a snowman – and he stopped in fright. Then he laughed a little goblin laugh.

"Ho, ho! You're only a snowman! You thought you could frighten me, standing there, watching. But you can't!"

He went into the hen house and came out with a bag full of eggs. Ha, ha! What a lovely lot!

He went up to the snowman. "Silly old snowman! Wouldn't you like to tell tales of me? But you can't!"

And then, to the Knobbly Goblin's horror, an arm shot out from the snowman and a deep voice said, "You just come along with me!"

He was held tightly in a big hand, and then he was shaken. "Put down those

eggs. You're a thief!" said the snowman.

The Knobbly Goblin was so frightened that he dropped the eggs. Luckily they fell into the snow and didn't break.

"P-p-p-please let me g-g-g-go," he begged. "Snowman, who are you? I've never met a live one before."

Mr Plod didn't answer. He took the

goblin to the police station – and there Knobbly saw that it was Mr Plod, the policeman, who had got him. Ooooooh!

Mr Plod went to see Mother Tuppeny the next day. "I've spanked the thief," he told her. "It was that Knobbly Goblin. I've sent him away, and I've made him pay a fine of ten golden pieces to me. Here they are! They will help to pay for all the eggs he has stolen. I was that snowman, Mother Tuppeny!"

"Oh – how I wish I'd seen you all dressed up!" cried Mother Tuppeny. "The children couldn't *think* what had happened to their snow-woman this morning. They were quite sad about her."

"You buy them some sweets," said Mr Plod. "And tell them how I put on the hat and shawl. They won't mind a bit then!"

They didn't, of course. They laughed when they heard about it.

As for Knobbly, he simply can't bear the sight of a snowman now!

# Old Mister Glue-Pot

Old Mister Glue-Pot was a gnome who lived in Pillywee Village, on the borders of Fairyland. He kept a paint shop and sold paint in pots, and also very sticky brown glue.

He made this glue himself, and it was so strong that just a touch of it would stick two broken pieces of a jar or dish together in a trice. Mister Glue-Pot had made a lot of money out of this very strong glue.

In fact, he had made such a lot of money that he really didn't bother very much about his shop. He put Snubby the pixie in charge of it, and then he went into his parlour, put his feet up on the mantelpiece, and slept peacefully.

Snubby was not a good shopkeeper. He played about too much. He painted the walls of the shop green and yellow, with blue spots – and will you believe it, Mister Glue-Pot never noticed! Then Snubby discovered the glue. What a game he had with it!

First of all he got some on his hands by mistake – and, dear me, whatever

Snubby touched stuck fast to him. He touched a newspaper and that stuck. He touched two pencils and those stuck! He touched Mister Glue-Pot's best Sunday hat and that stuck. Soon you could hardly see Snubby because so many things were sticking to him!

Snubby managed to unstick himself at last. He stood looking at Mister Glue-Pot's big barrel of glue and grinned. He would have a few jokes with that!

He peeled an orange and then carefully dabbed a spot of glue on each bit of peel. When no one was looking the naughty pixie slipped out of the shop and pressed each bit of peel on the pavement. They all stuck fast. Snubby knew that Mister Plod-Plod, the policeman, would come along that way in a few minutes' time – and old Plod-Plod would certainly try to pick up all those bits of peel!

"It will be fun to see him pulling at them," giggled the naughty pixie to himself. He pressed his snubby nose against the shop window and waited. Soon he heard the plod-plod-plod noise that the policeman's feet made. Up came Mister Plod-Plod and saw the orange peel.

"Now, who's been dropping orange peel about?" he said in his crossest voice. "It is forbidden to do such a thing!"

He looked all round but he could see no one. So Mister Plod-Plod stooped down to pick up all the bits himself – but they were stuck fast to the pavement! Plod-Plod pulled and tugged, and then stared at the peel in amazement. Was it magic? Why wouldn't it come off the pavement?

Plod-Plod took out his knife and cut all the peel away. He put it in his pocket and walked off, looking very puzzled and angry. Snubby laughed till his sides ached.

"That was a good trick!" he said. "Now what else shall I do?"

But before he could do anything else Mister Plod-Plod came back again and asked to see Mister Glue-Pot.

"Mister Glue-Pot," he said sternly, "did you know that someone has been using your glue to stick bits of orange peel to the pavement?"

"Dear me, no!" said Glue-Pot.

"Well, they have," said Plod-Plod. "Please see that you keep an eye on your glue-barrel, Glue-Pot."

"Certainly, certainly," said the old fellow, and he called Snubby to him. "Look after the glue-barrel very, very carefully," he said. Snubby grinned and nodded. He would look after it all right!

Now next door to Mister Glue-Pot's shop was a baker's shop, and outside the door was a very fine mat for people to wipe their feet on. Snubby thought it would be a great joke to dab some glue on it – and then everyone's feet would get stuck there. What fun that would be!

So that night he slipped out with a brush full of glue and daubed the whole mat with it. And you should have seen the muddle there was at the baker's next day!

Dame Trit-Trot and Mister Top-hat went to the baker's shop at the same time, and both trod on the mat together. That was all right – but when they tried to walk off it into the shop they couldn't. The mat went with them! Poor Dame Trit-Trot slipped and slid, trying to get her feet off the sticky mat, and Mister Top-hat suddenly lost his balance and sat down. That was worse than ever! It took the baker two hours to untangle Trit-Trot, Top-hat, and the mat.

How angry they all were! They marched into Mister Glue-Pot's shop and banged on the counter so loudly that Mister Glue-Pot, who was fast asleep in the parlour, woke up, leapt out of his chair, and trod on his poor cat. She scratched him hard and naughty Snubby laughed till he cried.

"If you don't look after your glue better, we shall punish you, Glue-Pot!" cried Trit-Trot, Top-hat, and the baker.

They told him about the sticky mat, and Glue-Pot was full of horror to think that his glue should be used for tricks like that.

"Just see you look after the glue-barrel even better than before," he said to Snubby. And Snubby grinned and said he would. But, the very next day, Snubby slipped across the road to the sweet-shop when it was empty, and dabbed the three chairs with the glue. Oh, what a dreadful thing to do!

That afternoon Snubby watched the people going in to buy sweets. He saw Mrs Lightfoot sit down on a chair. He saw Mister Tap-Tap. He saw the old brownie, Longbeard, sitting down too. They talked together for a little while till their sweets were ready – then they tried to get up to go.

But their chairs stuck to them! They ran out of the shop in horror, taking the chairs with them, though the shopkeeper shouted to them to bring them back. They ran down the street

with the chairs knocking behind them –
and they ran straight into Mister Plod-
Plod, the policeman. And it wasn't long
before he found that it was Mister Glue-
Pot's glue that had done the mischief
again.

He went straight to the paint-shop
and shouted for Mister Glue-Pot.

"Pack up your things, take your glue and leave Pillywee Village," he ordered. "We have had enough of these glue tricks, Mister Glue-Pot. Take this cheeky little pixie with you, for I shouldn't be surprised if he had done the mischief."

So poor Mister Glue-Pot and Snubby had to pack up and go. Snubby had to carry the barrel of glue on his back, for Mister Plod-Plod wouldn't let him leave it behind. So over the borders of Fairyland it was carried, and it's still somewhere about today.

Do you know what it is used for? Snubby and Glue-Pot sell it to the chestnut trees in the early spring, so that their buds can be painted with glue to prevent the frost from pinching them. Isn't that a good idea? Snubby paints each bud. You may see him if you look, but if you can't see him, pick a chestnut twig and feel how very strong Mister Glue-Pot's glue is. You *will* be surprised!

## Mr Stamp-About and the stick

Mr Stamp-About was in one of his tempers. "Who's taken my walking-stick?" he roared. "It's gone! Wait till I find out who's got it!" and he stamped his foot as hard as he could.

"Now, now, Mr Stamp-About, sir," said the milkman, who had just come to the door with his bottle of milk. "Don't take on so! You'll stamp a hole in the floor!"

"And why shouldn't I?" roared Stamp-About. "It's *my* floor, isn't it? Where's that walking-stick of mine? Have *you* seen it?"

"No, and if I had it wouldn't have been a *walking*-stick, I bet· it would have been a *running-away* stick, seeing you in such a temper!" grinned the milkman, and dodged as old Stamp-About threw a loaf of bread at him. "Oh, thank you, I'll take that loaf home to my hens!" And away he went, laughing.

What rages old Stamp-About did get into, to be sure!

Now, when Stamp-About went out that morning he felt quite peculiar without his stick. He didn't need it to help him to *walk* – he liked to use it to hit the heads off daisies or dandelions, or to shake at a shouting boy! He certainly missed his stick!

He went over the fields, grumbling to himself. "That rude milkman! And what was it the postman said to me yesterday – that it was a good thing they couldn't put me inside a cannon, or I'd explode and blow it to bits. Where's my stick? What CAN have happened to my stick?"

Now, as he came to the stile, he saw something beside it. It looked like a stick. In fact,, it *was* a stick! Stamp-About picked it up at once.

"Ha! A walking-stick! All by itself. And a good strong one, too. What's this on the top of the handle – a carving of some sort? A head – the head of a cheeky-looking fellow, too. Beautifully carved! I wonder who the stick belongs to?"

He tucked it under his arm and went off with it. If he heard that anyone had lost it he'd give it to them.

"But someone's taken mine, and I've got to have one for myself," thought Stamp-About. "And whoever owns this shouldn't have been careless enough to leave it about. Serve him right if he comes back and can't find it!"

He went home with the stick, feeling pleased with it. It was just the right size for him, very strong, and certainly that little head was most beautifully carved.

"Though I don't like the way it looks at me," thought Stamp-About. "Too cheeky for anything!" He stood it in

124

the corner of his room, and went to get himself a meal. Ah, there was plenty of that meat pie left. Good!

Just as he was putting it on the table, he heard a knock at the door, and a voice said, "Stamp-About, are you in? I've come to dinner with you!"

"That's old Cousin Gubbins!" thought Stamp-About crossly. "He'll eat half the pie! Well, I shan't open the door. Let him think I'm out."

He hid behind the cupboard door, in case Gubbins looked in at the window and saw him. Gubbins banged at the door again. And then Stamp-About was amazed to hear a thin, high voice calling out clearly, "Come in! He's at home!"

And Cousin Gubbins at once opened the door and came in. He looked round to see where the voice had come from, and saw Stamp-About behind the cupboard door.

"Hello, what are you doing there?" said Gubbins in astonishment.

"Hiding! *He, he!*" said the same little

high voice, and laughed and laughed.

Stamp-About was very angry. Now his cousin Gubbins had come in, after all ... and there was somebody in his kitchen being very, very annoying. Where did that voice come from? He simply couldn't imagine.

"I've come to dinner, Stamp-About," said Gubbins. "You've had three meals with me in three weeks – now it's my turn to have a meal with you."

"I've nothing to offer you," said Stamp-About, in a surly voice.

"Ooooooh! You've forgotten that meat pie!" said the little high voice. "Ooooh – you fibber!"

Stamp-About stared round the room. *WHO* had said that? There was nobody there except Stamp-About himself and his greedy cousin. He felt very uncomfortable. Was the voice real? Yes it must be, because Gubbins had heard it too.

"Ha – meat pie! Just what I feel like!" said Gubbins and sat down.

Stamp-About had to put the pie on the table, and the two made a good meal of it.

"There's a pudding in the larder," remarked the little high voice, after a bit. "*He, he* – you do look cross, Stamp-About!"

"Who's saying all these silly things?" roared Stamp-About, losing his temper.

"Do you suppose it's that stick over in the corner?" asked Gubbins, grinning. "The little head at the top has been winking at me ever since I sat down at the table."

"What!" cried Stamp-About, and stared over at the stick.

Yes – the little head was winking at him, too, and its small carved mouth smiled.

"Stamp-About stole me," said the stick.

"Oooh, what a story! I didn't!" said Stamp-About, angrily.

"Yes, you did. You should have taken me to the police station, but you didn't," said the little high voice. "I belong to Mr Spell-Maker. My word – whatever will he do to you when he knows you stole me from that stile? He was coming back for me, I know he was. He just left me there by mistake."

Stamp-About stared at the stick in horror. So it belonged to Mr Spell-Maker – and Mr Spell-Maker had just as bad a temper as Stamp-About.

"I'll take you to the police station at once," he said, and went over to the stick.

But it jumped into the air. "No!" it said. "I don't want to go there. I'll wait till my master finds out I'm here, and watch what he does to you. *He, he* – I once saw him turn a witch into an ice-cream."

Stamp-About was really scared. He snatched up the stick at once, and tucked it firmly under his arm. "You'd better come with me, Cousin Gubbins," he said.

"No, no," said Gubbins. "I'll just stay

and finish my meal. I'll look in the larder for the pudding."

Stamp-About groaned and went off to the police station. Before he got there the little carved wooden head under his arm had nipped him!

"Let me go!" it cried. "I'll nip you again!"

Stamp-About wasn't going to have that. He took out his handkerchief and tied it round the stick's carved head. "There!" he said. "Now you can't say a word!"

He took the stick to the police station. "I found it in a field," he said. "You'd better ask Mr Spell-Maker if it belongs to him. I don't want it. It's a rude stick, and spiteful, too!"

And away he went home, leaving the surprised policeman undoing the handkerchief from the stick's carved head. How amazed he was when the stick hit him on the shins and then tried to hop away. The policeman promptly locked it in a cell.

Stamp-About was most relieved to have left the stick behind. He hurried home, hoping to get there before Gubbins had eaten everything in the larder. But Gubbins had gone – and so had all the food except for half a loaf of stale bread!

Stamp-About went out to buy a cake for his tea. When he got back, he sat down for a snooze, and began to snore a little. He woke up very suddenly, to hear a little high voice say "Don't snore like that! I don't like it!"

And there was the stick again, standing by the fireplace, its little head glaring crossly at him.

"How did you get back here?" said Stamp-About, horrified.

"I didn't like the police station, so I just wriggled out between the bars of my cell," said the stick. "It was easy. Let me lean against your knee in front of the fire. I'll be nice and warm then."

"*No*," said Stamp-About, and got a rap on his leg that made him jump.

That stick could certainly be mean!

"I shall hit your knee-cap next if you try to move me," said the little carved head.

"You're a most extraordinary stick," Stamp-About said in amazement. "Did Mr Spell-Maker carve you?"

"Yes, then he rubbed a spell on my head so that I could talk," said the stick. "I wonder what he'll do to you when he knows *you've* got me!"

Stamp-About felt most alarmed again. He got up at once. "I'll throw you away in the river, and let you float for miles to the sea!" he said angrily.

The stick hopped away at once, over the kitchen floor, but Stamp-About chased it till he caught it. He tied a string to it and then, dragging it behind him so that it couldn't hit him, he set off to the river. *Splash*! He threw the stick into it, and sighed in relief. Why had he brought such a nasty, mean thing home with him? Well, that was the end of it.

He went back home and sat down to

finish his snooze in his arm chair – but would you believe it, he hadn't been asleep for more than half an hour when he felt something hit his knee. And then he felt something slithering all the way up him and down again. He opened his eyes in a hurry.

It was the carved stick back again! It was dripping wet and was wiping itself dry on Stamp-About's clothes.

"I jumped out of the river! I jumped out!" it said, in its little high voice. "It was cold and wet. Let me get into your warm pocket! Let me get behind your cosy waistcoat. What, you won't let me! Then I'll hit you!"

Stamp-About was really in despair. He stared at the wriggling stick in horror. Should he bury it? No, it might take root and grow into even more mean sticks. Should he put it into his dustbin? No, it would probably rattle the lid till someone let it out.

Well, then – there was only one thing left to do! He would take it back to

Mr Spell-Maker. He would be delighted to have it back, and Stamp-About would then have got rid of the annoying stick once and for all! He put the stick on the cushion in his chair and went to the cupboard. He found a nice long box, that had once had an umbrella in. He put some cotton wool in it and called to the stick.

"Here you are! I've made a nice, cosy, comfy bed for you, Stick! Cuddle down in this cotton wool, and you will soon be dry and warm!"

"Ah, now you're being sensible!" said the little wooden head, grinning, and the stick hopped over to the box. "Yes, it looks good. I'll lie down and get dry and warm."

The stick jumped into the long, narrow box and tucked itself into the wool. In a trice Stamp-About clapped the lid on and tied string tightly round it.

"Aha!" he said. "Got you! Now I'm taking you back to Mr Spell-Maker.

I've no doubt you will be very glad to hear that. You're not going to have any chance of rapping my shins though. You can stay quite still in this box!"

But that's just what the carved stick wouldn't do! It jiggled about, rapped against the lid, and cried out loudly in its high little voice. As Stamp-About carried the box down the road, everyone stared in amazement.

"Whatever *have* you got in that box?" said old Dame Hurry-By. "If it's some poor animal, you let it out at once!"

Stamp-About didn't stop until he came to Mr Spell-Maker's little pointed house on the top of the hill. He rapped on the door. "Mr Spell-Maker! I've brought back your stick!"

Old Mr Spell-Maker put his head out of the window. "For goodness sake! I left it by the stile because I never wanted to see it again. It's a perfect nuisance of a stick. *I* don't want it!"

He slammed the window. Stamp-

About heard the stick laughing and, in a rage, he opened the front door and flung the box inside. Then he slammed the door and went off down the hill at top speed. He was *not* going to have that stick again.

But soon he heard a little high voice shouting breathlessly to him. "Wait! Wait! Mr Spell-Maker says you can have me. I slid out of the letter-box. Wait! Wait!"

But Stamp-About didn't wait. He rushed home and went to shut himself in his garden-shed.

No sooner was he in the shed than he saw his own dear old stick, carved with a dog's head on top, the one he had lost! Well, well, well, of course, he had left it in the shed the day before. He picked it up in delight and just at that very moment the other stick came rapping at the shed door.

Stamp-About opened it, his own stick in his hand. In came the other stick, complaining bitterly. "Why did you

136

leave me? I've come to live with *you* now. Oh, what's that?"

"My *own* stick!" roared Stamp-About. "See the dog's head on top? Do you want it to chase you and bite you? *Grrrrrrrr!*"

Stamp-About growled so exactly like a dog that the first stick hopped away hurriedly down the garden path.

"No, no!" it cried. "No, no!"

And that was the last time that Stamp-About ever heard the carved head's little high voice.

Goodness knows where the stick went to. Stamp-About is so afraid it may come back that he's paying Mr Spell-Maker to put special magic on his own stick, to make it bark. That will scare away any other stick – and burglars, too. I wouldn't mind a stick like that myself! It would really be very useful!

## Mister Quink's garden

O nce upon a time, not very long ago, Mr Brown took his family for a day in the country. There were Mrs Brown, the mother, Annie Brown, the little girl, and Tommy Brown, the little boy.

"We'll all go, every one of us," said Mr Brown. "The country is lovely now. We shall enjoy it. Take enough food for the whole day, Mummy."

So Mrs Brown cut ham sandwiches and tomato sandwiches, and packed them into cardboard boxes. She took two bottles of lemon barley water. She packed four oranges and four bananas into a basket with the bottles. She took a large tin of fruit salad, and four cardboard plates and spoons to

eat it with. And last of all she took four bars of chocolate and a bag of peppermints.

So you can see that the Brown family meant to have a good feast. It was a lovely day when they set off in the bus. The sun shone brightly. The sky was as blue as the bluebells that were beginning to peep in the woods. The birds in the hedges sang merrily and the banks were yellow with primroses.

Mrs Brown was happy. She sat in the bus and looked at everything. Mr Brown was happy too. The children looked out for an ice-cream man with his van, for they each had some money to spend and they wanted ice-cream. They were happy too.

They got off the bus at last and walked into the woods. The sun was so hot that they were glad of the shade. Tommy and Annie danced on in front, shouting to their mother to look at the bluebells. Mr and Mrs Brown carried the bags and basket.

"Look for a nice place to sit, Annie," called Mrs Brown.

Presently they found one. It was the prettiest place in the wood – and, although they did not know it, it was really the garden belonging to Mister Quink, the old brownie. He lived in the old oak tree under whose branches the Brown family sat. He had a close-fitting door in the trunk of the tree and a small window with a tiny curtain of moss. Nobody ever knew he lived there – except the little folk of course – because Mister Quink never showed himself to ordinary people.

Now Mister Quink was very proud of his garden and he worked there every night. There was a tiny stream running through it, and he had planted flowers neatly along each side. He had arranged cushions of moss here and there in his garden too, so that his friends might sit on them when they came to visit him. He had three patches of bluebells, the finest in the wood – and one special secret plant which always grew a *white* bluebell, which, as you know, is a very lucky flower.

Mister Quink had made a little bower of honeysuckle leaves in one corner, and a nook of violets grew close by, so that whoever sat in the nook could smell the sweet scent of the hidden violets. Everything in the garden was neat and tidy and beautiful.

No wonder the Browns thought it was lovely! Mr and Mrs Brown sat down under the tree and put their basket and bags by them. They didn't know they were in a brownie's garden, because Mister Quink had no fence or wall or hedge round it. The children wanted to have something to eat at once.

"Well, we'll have our dinner now," said Mrs Brown, and she began to unpack the things. Soon they were all munching happily. They drank the lemon barley water. It was delicious.

"Let's put the bottles up over there and throw stones at them," said

Mr Brown. "We'll break them."

"But won't the broken pieces be dangerous?" said Mrs Brown.

"Pooh! Who will ever come here?" said Mr Brown.

So they set up the bottles and threw stones at them, and soon the two bottles were smashed to bits, and pieces of glass lay all over the little dell. Mr Brown unfolded his newspaper. "Now I'm going to have a rest," he said. "Don't disturb me, children."

Little by little the lovely garden belonging to Mister Quink began to look dreadful. The brownie peeped out of his tiny window in the oak tree and saw with dismay all that was happening.

He saw Mrs Brown peel oranges for the children and throw the peel on the grass. He saw the children eating bananas and throwing the skins at one another – for they were not very well-behaved children. He saw Mr Brown throw his banana skin into the honeysuckle bower.

The Brown family stayed there all the afternoon. It was so peaceful, and the birds sang so sweetly. They had their tea there too – and soon it was time to go home.

Mrs Brown looked round at the mess, and couldn't help feeling a bit sorry about it.

"Are there any litter bins or baskets anywhere?" she asked. "Perhaps we ought to put this mess into one."

"There aren't any, Mummy," said Tommy. "This is quite a wild part of the wood. I don't suppose anyone comes here but us. All the same, our teacher always tells us at school not to spoil the country – do you suppose we ought to take our rubbish back home with us?"

"I'm not carrying back all that litter," said Mr Brown at once. He was rather a selfish man. "Leave it here. No one will ever know."

"Mummy, let's take these bluebells home with us," cried Annie. "And let's dig up these primroses and violets by the root, and some of this moss. They'll look lovely in our garden at home!"

So they dug up Mister Quink's finest primroses and violets and moss, and picked all his bluebells – and then they found the lucky white bluebell! So they dug up its bulb and put that in the basket too. Then home they went.

Mister Quink opened his front door and crept out. When he saw his beautiful garden scattered with broken glass, orange peel, banana skins, cardboard boxes, empty bags, chocolate paper and sheets of newspaper – when he saw his lovely plants gone and his moss spoilt, he sat down on a stone and cried big tears.

But when he found his white bluebell gone he was very angry! He called a meeting of all the brownies in the wood and they came to see his spoilt garden.

Most of them had complaints and grumbles too.

"Some people left all their horrid paper bags in my field the other day," said Nod, an old brownie.

"And some boys threw broken bottles into my stream, and I scratched my foot when I paddled there," said Doolin, a small, bright-eyed brownie.

"But these Browns are the worst of the lot," said Mister Quink fiercely. "Look at this mess! Whatever shall I do with it?"

"The Browns have a neat little garden," said Hoodle, a sharp-eyed brownie who travelled a good deal. "As all this mess belongs to them, why not take it back to them and put it into their own garden?"

"That's a good idea!" said all the brownies at once. "They don't seem to mind litter and rubbish and mess – so maybe they won't bother about broken bottles and papers and peel in their own garden."

"I can give them about six old newspapers I've picked up from my field at one time and another," said Nod.

"And I can give them a sackful of broken glass," said Doolin.

"We'll go tonight and dump everything in the Browns' garden," said everyone. "Just the thing! How pleased they will be to get such a nice lot of rubbish back!"

So that night seven brownies all made their way from the wood and rode on the back of the midnight owl who flies to and from the town. When they got to the Browns' garden they landed on the grass and opened their sacks.

They shook out the glass all over the neat lawn. They threw the newspapers where the wind could blow them around. They scattered the paper and boxes and peel and skin here and there. And just as they were going, Mister Quink stopped short and pointed to something.

"Look!" he said. "My lucky white bluebell! I must take that back with me."

"And see – here's a lupin plant just flowering!" said Nod. "I haven't one of those at home. As the Browns took your flowers, Quink, they probably wouldn't mind us taking theirs. I *must* have that lupin!"

In a few minutes the brownies were digging up all the finest things in the Browns' garden, and then off they went again on the owl, their sacks empty of rubbish but full now of lovely plants. The brownies were delighted.

In the morning, when Mr Brown awoke and looked out of the window to see what sort of a day it was, he got *such* a shock! His garden was a perfect wreck! His favourite plants were gone – his lawn was scattered with broken glass – and all kinds of rubbish blew about or lay on the beds.

"Just look at that!" said Mr Brown fiercely. "Just look at that. Now who's done that, I should like to know!"

Mrs Brown jumped out of bed and gazed at the dreadful garden. Tears came into her eyes, for she loved her little garden. "Oh, how could anyone be so horrid!" she said.

Tommy and Annie were angry too. "What a terrible mess," said Annie. "Why don't people clear up their litter properly instead of throwing it into *our* garden?"

Well, Mr Brown told the policeman, and the policeman wrote a lot of things down in his notebook and said he would keep a watch on the garden and see it didn't happen again. And Tommy and Annie spent the whole morning clearing up the mess and making the garden neat. Mr Brown had to buy more plants in place of the ones that had gone, and he was very angry about it.

Well, will you believe it, although the policeman watched carefully the next night, *some*body he didn't see came and emptied all sorts of rubbish in the Browns' garden again! It was most extraordinary because although the policeman saw the rubbish being thrown about the garden he couldn't see who was throwing it!

The brownies were invisible to him, for he didn't believe in fairies. He was frightened and ran all the way back to the police station.

And do you know, the brownies still come every other night or so and give to the Browns all the rubbish that people leave about the countryside. Their garden is a dreadful sight and they can't do anything about it.

Annie is beginning to wonder if it *can* be the little folk who are doing it – and she wishes the Browns hadn't been so untidy in the wood that day!

"I shall put up a notice to say we're sorry and won't spoil the country again," said Annie to herself. "Then the little folk will stop bringing us rubbish."

So she is going to do that tonight – and then the brownies will have to choose someone else's garden. I hope it won't be yours! But I'm sure you are not like the Browns, are you? You know how to behave when you go to the country, so *your* garden will be safe!

# The runaway cheeses

One day a man of Gotham took his cheeses in a bag to sell at Nottingham market. He slung them over his back and started off, whistling merrily as he went.

Now when he got to the hill that leads to Nottingham Bridge, and was about to go down it, one of the cheeses fell out of his bag and rolled away down the hill. The man of Gotham stood and watched it in surprise.

"You're a fine fellow of a cheese!" he cried. "I see you know the way to market as well as I do! Well, if you can run there alone, I do not need to carry you. Perhaps all the cheeses can run by themselves to the market, and I shall have no burden to carry!"

The silly fellow took out another cheese from his bag and rolled it away down the hill. Then he took a third and sent that rolling away too. And soon his bag was quite empty, for each one of his cheeses he sent rolling down the hill.

Some of them ran into bushes and

153

stayed there. Some knocked against stones and were shattered to pieces. Others fell into rabbit holes and scared the bunnies. Not one of them reached the bottom of the hill.

When the man of Gotham had sent his last cheese rolling down the hillside, he put his hands to his mouth and shouted after them. "I command each one of you cheeses to meet me near the market!" he called at the top of his voice. Then down the hill he went himself, glad that his bag was no longer heavy, and thinking himself a mighty clever fellow to have sent his cheeses to meet him.

In half an hour's time he came to the market. He looked about for his cheeses, but could not see them. He waited the whole morning, but still the cheeses did not come. He looked in this corner for them and in that, but not a sign of them did he see.

Midday came and went. Still there were no cheeses. The afternoon came, and the sun moved slowly towards the west. The man of Gotham still watched for his cheeses, but at last, when the market was closed for the day, he gave up his watching, and began to ask his friends about them.

He went to a farmer and asked him if he had seen his cheeses come to market.

"Who should have brought them?" asked the farmer.

"Oh, they know the way themselves," said the man of Gotham.

But the farmer shook his head, and said, no, he had seen no cheeses that day. Then the man went to a pig-dealer.

"Have you seen my cheeses come to market?" he asked.

"Who should have brought them?" asked the pig-dealer.

"Oh, they know the way themselves," said the man of Gotham.

The pig-dealer stared and laughed, and said, no, he had seen no cheeses that day.

In vain the man went to all his

friends. They each gave the same answer. None of them had seen the cheeses come to market.

"Now bad luck to them!" said the man of Gotham, crossly. "I was afraid, when I saw them run so fast down the hill, that they would roll beyond the market, and not stop there to meet me. They must have run right through Nottingham and gone on to York. What senseless cheeses to do such a thing!"

He wondered what he should do, and he decided to hire a horse and ride on the road to York to see if he could catch up with his cheeses. So he paid a man for a horse, and mounted him. Off he went at a gallop to seek for his cheeses.

But although he kept a sharp lookout on the road for his rolling cheeses he saw none of them. When he came to York they were not there either, though the man of Gotham inquired of everyone he saw.

And to this day he does not know where his cheeses are!

## Ma Rubbalong deals with Loll-About

"**M**a!" called little Rubbalong from where he sat mending boots and shoes. "Here comes Loll-About."

He knew his mother couldn't bear Loll-About. He leaned against everything. He couldn't seem to stand up straight. He was always tired. Ma Rubbalong usually lost her temper when Loll-About came to bring boots to be mended.

"Oho – so it's Loll-About again, is it?" she said, drying her hands quickly. "Well, I said I'd teach him a lesson next time he came along if he hadn't learnt to stand up straight and take his hands out of his pockets."

"He's got some boots with him – he's coming here," said little Rubbalong in delight. "Have you got that lesson ready for him, Ma?"

"I'm getting it ready!" said Ma, briskly, and little Rubbalong saw that she was rubbing the table and the chairs and the doorway and the dresser, in fact every bit of furniture in the room, with a magic duster. What spell had she muttered into it? Rubbalong couldn't imagine!

Loll-About came in at the door. His boots were slung round his neck, and his hands were in his pockets. He slouched as usual.

"Stand up straight and take your hands out of your pockets!" said Ma Rubbalong, sharply. "Have you no manners?"

Loll-About sulkily took his hands out of his pockets. He stood up for a moment, and then he leaned against the table.

It went over with a crash. Loll-About

stared in alarm. Ma Rubbalong gave a snort. "Look at that – did you *have* to loll against the table and knock it over? Stand up straight, I tell you! And pick up all those potatoes that have rolled off on to the floor."

Loll-About set down his boots and picked up the potatoes. He felt rather tired after so much bending, and leaned against the dresser.

Over it went with a tremendous crash! Loll-About almost jumped out of his skin. So did little Rubbalong. Nothing was broken, which seemed rather strange to Rubbalong. Ma spoke angrily to Loll-About.

"*Now* look what you've done! What do you want to go and knock over my dresser for? Lolling about like that!"

"Ma Rubbalong – I'm very sorry," said Loll-About, scared and alarmed at what he had done. "I'm so glad nothing's broken. I'll put the dresser up again for you."

He put it up, with much panting and

puffing. Nobody helped him. Rubbalong went on cobbling shoes and boots and Ma stirred something on the stove.

Loll-About was out of breath when he had heaved the dresser into place. He leaned against Ma's old rocking-chair, panting.

Over went the chair as if it were a skittle – and this time Loll-About went down with it, and bumped himself hard.

"Well!" said Ma Rubbalong, angrily. "What do you suppose you're doing this morning, Loll-About? Do you make a habit of pushing things over?"

"No, Ma, no," said poor Loll-About, getting up in a hurry and putting the chair on its rockers again. "It won't happen again. I won't go near your furniture. I just can't understand it."

He went to stand in the doorway, really afraid of going near a chair or table now. He leaned against it, of course – he just simply couldn't seem to stand up straight by himself.

And will you believe it, the door fell

off its hinges on to the floor! Loll-About stared at it in horror. "Ma Rubbalong! Don't blame me, please don't blame me!" he cried, in alarm. "I only *just* leaned against the doorway – how was I to know the door was so loose?"

"Pick it up, and put it back on its hinges," commanded Ma Rubbalong, and poor Loll-About had to heave the heavy door into place, and spend half an hour putting it right.

"And let me warn you, Loll-About, that if you push my wall down, I'll throw you out of the window," said Ma. "Bless us all – there you go again!"

Poor Loll-About – he had leaned against the broom cupboard, quite tired out with his hard work – and down that went, too, of course! Brooms, brushes, and pans flew out, crashing round him.

Little Rubbalong bent over his cobbling, laughing till the tears ran down his cheeks. Clever old Ma! What shocks she was giving lazy Loll-About! Now he would have to spend twenty minutes standing the cupboard up again and putting everything back.

Ma Rubbalong disappeared into the street outside for a minute while Loll-About was busy with the cupboard. When little Rubbalong saw that she was rubbing the lamp post outside with her magic duster, he almost fell off his stool with laughter.

"You'd better go," said Ma, when Loll-About had put everything back into the cupboard. "If you knock one more thing over I shall most certainly throw you out of the window. I can feel it coming!"

Loll-About went out in alarm. He felt very, very tired now. He came to the lamp post and leaned himself against it for a rest.

CRASH! Down it went, and Loll-About yelled in fright. And, oh my, oh my, there was Mr Plod the policeman coming along, looking very angry indeed.

"What do you want to go about pushing lamp posts down for?" yelled

163

Mr Plod. "You wait till I catch you!"

But Loll-About didn't wait. He ran off faster than he had run for years. When Mr Plod came up he found little Rubbalong and Ma rolling round the kitchen, almost crying with laughter. He laughed, too, when he heard the joke.

"Well, maybe Loll-About will stop his lazy lolling ways now," said Mr Plod. "I could think of a few other people to use your spell on, Ma, too!"

So could I! I expect you could, as well!

## Mr Goofy's spell

M r Goofy was a brownie who didn't use his brains much. One fine October day he got too near a bonfire in his garden and burnt his beard off!

He was very upset. He looked at himself in the glass and groaned. "It's the dear Princess's party next week – and here am I with no beard! Who ever heard of a brownie without a beard?"

He certainly did look funny. His friend Jinky came in to see him. "Good gracious, Goofy," he said, "you'll have to do something about your beard! You can't possibly go to the party looking like that."

"Well, I can't grow a beard in a week, can I!" cried Goofy. "I wish I knew a spell that would make it grow quickly."

"Why not go to Dame Busy," said Jinky. "She's got spells for everything. She's very, very clever."

"Yes, I'll go to her," said Goofy, and he put on his hat and went. Dame Busy didn't think much of Goofy. She thought he was stupid and lazy-minded and sometimes rude, and she had often thought that a sharp lesson would be good for him. She looked at him as he came hurrying through her door.

"Why, Goofy, I haven't seen you move so quickly for some time," she said. "What's the matter? And what *have* you done with your beard?"

Goofy explained all about it. "And, you see," he said, "I want a spell to make it grow quickly."

"Well, I know a spell for that," said Dame Busy. "But it's expensive. Very expensive."

"Oh," said Goofy. "How much? I simply must have it."

"It will cost you a whole bag of your

apples," said Dame Busy, who had no apples at all in her garden.

"All right," said Goofy, with a sigh. "Now tell me the spell."

"I'll make it for you," said Dame Busy, "and when it's made you can tell me if you still want it or not."

She took down a green glass bowl. She poured boiling water into it. The steam rose up to the ceiling. Then she got a ripe poppy head and scattered the seeds into the water as if she was shaking pepper from a pot.

Next she shredded a scarlet toadstool into the bowl, and then took four black hairs from the tail of Cinders, her cat. Those went in, too, and after that three dewdrops strung together on a spider's thread. They made a little hissing noise.

Then Dame Busy muttered a few magic words that Goofy tried his hardest to hear. The steaming water in the glass bowl at once turned bright yellow, and began to bubble instead of steam.

"Now," said Dame Busy, looking hard at Goofy, "listen well to me, Goofy. This is a powerful spell for growing beards very quickly indeed. All it needs now is to be well stirred with a cuckoo's feather. Then smear it on your face and wait for two days."

"That's easy!" said Goofy joyfully. "I'll go and find a cuckoo this very day and ask him for a feather. And if I can't find a cuckoo, I could look for his nest and perhaps I might find an old feather there. Would an old feather do, Dame Busy?"

"If you can find a cuckoo's nest, certainly an old feather will do," said Dame Busy. "Now, think hard, Goofy – I have made you the spell to grow a beard quickly – and I have told you what to stir it with. Do you still want the spell?"

"Oh, *yes!*" said Goofy at once. "Of course I do. I'll take it now, please, and I'll bring you the apples at midday."

Dame Busy poured the bubbling

yellow spell into a big bottle and gave it to Goofy, with a little smile. "Well, there you are!" she said. "It'll be your fault if your beard doesn't grow quickly, Goofy!"

Goofy was pleased. He danced home. He counted out a hundred good apples and put them into a sack. Then he took them to Dame Busy's house.

After that he danced off to find a cuckoo. It was a beautiful autumn day. Blackberries were ripening in the woods. The leaves were turning colour. Goofy felt happy as he danced along. He listened for a cuckoo to call. Everyone knew the loud cuckooing of the big cuckoo-bird.

But he didn't hear it at all. How strange! He hunted the wood from end to end, but he could find no cuckoo at all, nor even hear one.

"What are you looking for, Goofy?" asked a bright-eyed elf.

"A cuckoo," said Goofy. "I've hunted everywhere and I can't find one."

"Silly Goofy!" said the elf. "Don't you know the cuckoos fly away south long before this? I haven't heard a cuckoo since July!"

"Well, now I come to think of it I suppose I haven't either," said Goofy. "How stupid of me! I forgot they flew away south so early."

He went all though the wood again, and this time he hunted for a cuckoo's nest. How he hunted! But he could only find the nests of blackbirds and thrushes. He wondered what a cuckoo's nest was like. He really must find one or he wouldn't be able to get a feather to stir the spell.

"Goofy, what are you hunting for *now*?" asked the elf.

"A cuckoo's nest," said Goofy gloomily. "But there doesn't seem to be a single one anywhere."

The elf laughed. "Goofy, how silly you are! Don't you know that cuckoos *never* build nests? They put their eggs into the nests of other birds."

"Do they really?" said Goofy, astonished. "Well, to think I didn't know that." Then his face grew very long. "Oh my! Then that spell's no good to me! The cuckoos have all gone away, so I can't ask any of them for a feather – and they don't build nests, so I can't find an old feather there! Now my beard won't grow, and I shan't be able to go to the party. Boo-hoo, woo-hoo-hoo!"

"Poor Goofy!" said the elf, laughing. "You never use your eyes or your ears or your brains, do you? Well, it serves you right to have a trick played on you like that. Perhaps you'll think a bit harder in the future."

Well, perhaps he will – and perhaps he won't! Do tell me, would *you* have gone looking for a cuckoo, too, and hunted for its nest?

# The astonishing party

All the children in Hawthorn Village were excited. They had been invited to a party.

And Dame Twinkle was giving it! Dame Twinkle was a marvellous person, as magic as can be. She knew all kinds of tricks and jokes and spells. She could tell you what the weather would be on Wednesday week. She could tell you where to find the first violet and the biggest bluebell. She knew where the juiciest blackberries grew and the finest nuts.

She was jolly and friendly and amusing – and how she could scold if she was cross! It would be exciting to go to a party given by Dame Twinkle.

"You'll have to behave yourselves," said Miss Brown, their teacher. "Dame Twinkle doesn't like naughty or ill-mannered children. So be careful!"

Well, the children all dressed themselves up nicely and went up the hill to Dame Twinkle's cottage. Its windows were like her name – they twinkled in the sun, and the garden was bright with flowers. It was a sunny day, so the children hoped they could play in the garden.

Dame Twinkle welcomed them. "Good afternoon, Annie – and Benny – and Connie – and Dick – and Elsie and all of you! How nice you look!"

"I hope she's got a good tea!" whispered Percy to Connie. Dame Twinkle had sharp ears and she heard what Percy said. She frowned.

'Now," she said, "this will be rather a funny party, so be careful how you behave. There is a good bit of magic about the garden this afternoon!"

First of all Dame Twinkle gave the children coloured balloons to play with. That was fun! They threw them into the air, punched them when they came down again, and had a lovely time.

Then Gladys threw her balloon too near a holly bush – and it caught on a prickle and burst. Gladys burst too – into tears! She sobbed and she wailed, and Dame Twinkle came running up in alarm.

"My dear child, what have you done – broken a leg or an arm?"

"My balloon's *burst*," wailed Gladys.

"Now, my dear, you are behaving like a little goose," said Dame Twinkle firmly. And then a very strange thing happened.

Gladys turned into a goose! She did, really. She still wore her own clothes, but she was a goose. She opened her beak to wail, but she cackled instead.

"Oh – it's the magic in the garden!" cried the children in delight. "Oh, Dame Twinkle, Gladys behaved like a goose and she is one! Goosie-goosie-Gladys!"

"Well, well – you can't say I didn't warn you!" said Dame Twinkle. "Cheer up, Gladys, the magic will go sooner or later!"

"Dame Twinkle, do you like the beautiful dress my auntie gave me?" said Polly, a very vain little girl, running up to Dame Twinkle. She twisted herself round to show the dress.

"My!" said Dame Twinkle, "you're as proud as a peacock, Polly, aren't you!"

And, dear me, Polly changed into a

peacock! There she stood, dressed in her clothes still, but with a magnificent tail spread out behind her – a very fine peacock indeed. She opened her beak to cry, but made an ugly screeching noise instead.

Micky stared, afraid. He ran into a corner, and tried to hide. He was always afraid of everything. Elsie pointed her finger at him. "Look at Micky! He's as timid as a *mouse*!"

And Micky at once turned into a mouse, of course – a nice big one, dressed in shorts and jersey, with a woffly nose, and a long tail. He had to carry it because he fell over it. He squeaked when *he* wanted to talk.

"I say – we'd better be careful," said Bobby in alarm. "There's an awful lot of magic about today!"

"Come and have tea, come and have tea!" cried Dame Twinkle, and the children rushed indoors. They saw such a fine tea, and Percy's eyes gleamed. He was a very greedy little boy. He sat himself down opposite the biggest plate of buns.

How he ate! He stuffed himself full of buns and sandwiches, cakes and biscuits, and the other children stared at him in disgust.

"You're as greedy as a pig, Percy," said Bobby. And, dear me – Percy was immediately a pig! There he sat, grunting, his little piggy eyes staring all round, and his curly tail sticking out at the back of him. The children laughed. Percy really did look very funny.

The children were told to help themselves, and they did – all except Dick, who waited to be asked. Nobody asked him what he wanted, of course, and he felt very hurt, and sat with his plate empty for a long time.

He saw all the other children eating the things he liked. Soon his eyes filled with tears and he cried.

"What's the matter?" said Dame Twinkle. "Do you feel ill, Dick?"

"No. But, oh, nobody looks after me,

nobody offers me anything, and I've had hardly any tea!" wailed Dick.

"Well, didn't I tell you all to help yourselves?" said Dame Twinkle impatiently. "What a little donkey you are!"

And he was just that – a dear little grey donkey, with big, long ears that twitched, and a voice that said "Hee-haw!" very loudly! The other children laughed and petted him.

"Shall I get you some thistles and carrots for your tea?" said John. "Dear little Dickie Donkey!"

John slipped away from the table and went into the field beyond the garden. He came back with an armful of thistles which he pushed under poor Dick's nose.

"Now, John, now," said Dame Twinkle, "you really are a monkey to go and get those thistles!"

And, of course, as soon as she said that, John *was* a monkey! A nice brown monkey with a grinning face, and a long tail that was very useful to him, for he at once jumped up to the lamp, and hung downwards from it by his tail!

The children squealed. What an astonishing party! Who would change next? Really, it was so sudden, you never knew what your neighbour was going to turn into from one minute to the next.

Fred pushed some food into his pocket, hoping that no one would see him. Then he could eat cakes and biscuits in bed that night. But Dame Twinkle's sharp eyes did see him. She pounced on him at once!

"Now, Fred, you take those things out of your pocket at once! None of your artful ways here! You're as sly as a fox, the way you behave!"

And a fox he was, a beautiful red fox, with a pointed nose, sharp ears and a wonderful tail. The children looked at him.

"Well – Fred always was a bit like a fox!" said Pam. "He had such a very sharp little nose, hadn't he!"

"Really, this party seems to be turning into a zoo!" said Dame Twinkle, looking round at the birds and animals there. "There are only a few of you left that are boys and girls. Well, well, well!"

She started them off on a hopping race round the garden, whilst she went to wash up the tea-things. Hop-hop-hop they went down the path.

"Fanny's cheating!" cried Annie. "She put her other foot to the ground."

"You're cheating yourself!" cried John. "Look at you – two feet on the ground now!"

"So are you, John!" said Benny, and he gave him a push. John pushed back. The other children hopped quickly ahead. The boys rushed after them to stop them.

"Begin again, begin again!" cried Annie. "It's not fair! Benny, don't tug at my dress. You'll tear it."

Annie pushed John, and he pushed

her back. "You look as cross as a bear!" he said.

And Annie became a bear – a nice, soft, fat little bear, with tears rolling down its nose because John had pushed it. She opened her big mouth to wail, but only a grunt came out.

Then the children began to quarrel again about who had won the hopping match. Benny knocked John over. Elsie pushed Benny. They screamed and behaved very badly indeed.

Dame Twinkle came running out, looking cross. Couldn't these children amuse themselves even for ten minutes without squealing and fighting?

"Now, now!" she cried. "Stop fighting like cats and dogs! I'm ashamed of you!"

Well! All those who were squabbling at once became cats and dogs – and there they were, tails swinging or wagging, voices meowing or barking, a most astonished lot of creatures!

Dame Twinkle looked at them all. "A goose – a donkey – a mouse – a peacock

– a pig – a fox – a monkey – a bear – and any amount of cats and dogs!" she said. "What a party! Well, I meant this to be a children's party, not a zoo meeting. You'd better all go home, and I'll save the supper lemonade and biscuits till tomorrow morning. Then, if you are nicely behaved boys and girls again, you can come and get them."

So the donkey, the goose, the mouse, the peacock, the fox, the pig, the monkey, the bear and the cats and dogs all went rather sadly home, wondering what their mothers would say when they saw them.

But you will be glad to know that as soon as they reached their own gates they turned back into boys and girls again, much to their delight. So maybe they will get the lemonade and biscuits tomorrow after all.

What an astonishing party! Do you think *you* would have turned into a bird or animal if you had been there? And if so – *what* would you have been?

# Mr Stamp-About again

M r Stamp-About went to stay with his aunt, Miss Prim, and his uncle, Mr Hearty. They asked him for Christmas, and said he could stay until the New Year was in.

"Thanks very much," said Mr Stamp-About, pleased. "I should have been all alone if you hadn't asked me. I'll come with pleasure."

He packed up his things. Mr Cheery from next door helped him to carry them to the station.

"Now you have a good time, Stamp-About," he said, "and just remember that when you stay with people you have to put on your best behaviour – so no stamping about and shouting!"

"Don't you talk to me like that!" said Stamp-About, glaring. "Do you suppose I don't know how to behave?"

"Well, that's just what I do suppose," said Cheery. "*I* heard you stamping round the kitchen roaring at your cat this morning. She came flying out of the window like a streak of lightning!"

Stamp-About opened his mouth to roar at Cheery, but the train came in and roared even louder. He got in and Cheery banged the door. "Happy Christmas!" he said, "and don't forget to make some good resolutions for the New Year!"

Well, Stamp-About really did have a lovely Christmas and enjoyed himself very much. He stayed till the New Year, and on New Year's Eve, when he was in bed, he made all kinds of very good resolutions, just as you do. You know what good resolutions are, of course – you make up your mind to do this and do that all through the New Year, and not to do the things you know you shouldn't.

"I shall keep my temper," thought Stamp-About. "I shall not shout or yell. I shall not stamp my feet. I shall not be rude. I shall, in fact, be quite a different person. Dear me, how interesting it will be."

He fell asleep feeling pleased and happy. How easy it was to make good resolutions – and what a fine lot he had made.

Now, the next day Mr Cheery came along to help him back home with his luggage, and he brought his cheeky little nephew, Smarty, with him. Mr Stamp-About looked at Smarty, and he didn't like him.

"Well, Smarty," said Miss Prim, "this is New Year's Day. I am sure you have made all kinds of good resolutions."

"Yes, Miss Prim," said Smarty. "But I bet Mr Stamp-About hasn't."

"No, I don't suppose he has," said Mr Hearty. "Stamp-About, I've never known you make a good New Year's resolution yet! You'd have got rid of that bad temper of yours if you had!"

"*Ha ha!*" said Mr Cheery, "why, I wouldn't know old Stamp-About without his temper! He loses it so often that I really think he must spend his days finding it again! *Ha ha!*"

"That's not funny," said Mr Stamp-About, glaring at him.

"*I* think it's funny," said Smarty, and laughed so much that he fell over. "You want to keep your temper tied up like a dog, Mr Stamp-About. Then you wouldn't lose it. That could be one of your good resolutions – buy lead and collar for temper, and tie it up. *Ha ha ha!*"

"If Stamp-About wanted to make any good resolutions I could tell him plenty," said Uncle Hearty. "Now, now – don't look so upset, Stamp-About. We're only teasing you."

"Then don't," said Stamp-About, going very red in the face. "I don't mind telling you that I've made more good resolutions this New Year than all of you people put together. So there!"

Everyone laughed. Cheery poked him in the ribs. "Don't boast, old fellow – and, anyway, I can guess what your resolutions are – shout at the cat, yell at the dog, moan at everybody, and. . . ."

"How *dare* you say that!" yelled Mr Stamp-About, losing his temper very suddenly indeed. "Poking your great silly nose into my affairs! Telling me not to boast! *I* don't boast. You're the one who boasts. And as for that silly nephew of yours, if he doesn't take that stupid grin off his face, I'll make him stand outside in the cold!"

"What behaviour!" said Miss Prim, shocked. "Apologise to Smarty, Stamp-About."

"Certainly not!" roared Stamp-About, and he stamped his foot so hard that all the ornaments on the mantelpiece jumped. "Getting at me like this! I won't have it. No, I won't."

He stamped round the room, fuming, and shook his big fist right under

Smarty's nose. "*Grrrrrrr!*" he roared.

"Now, now," said Miss Prim, shocked, "aren't you forgetting this is New Year? What a pity you didn't make a few really good resolutions, Stamp-About!"

Stamp-About went purple. He roared at his aunt. "I tell you I *did* make some good resolutions. Plenty. More than anybody. *Ha!* You don't believe me, do you?"

"Well, tell us them, then maybe we *will* believe you," said Cheery.

"Right!" shouted Stamp-About, with an enormous frown. "Well, here they are – and jolly good ones, too. I made up my mind to keep my temper. And not to shout or yell. Not to stamp my feet. And not to be rude. So there! *Now* do you believe me?"

And he stamped his foot again, and made the clock suddenly strike twelve before it ought to.

Everyone began to laugh. Cheery pointed his finger at the angry Stamp-About. "I'll die of laughing, Stamp-

About, I really will! Did you forget that good resolutions have to be *kept*? Don't you know that. . . ."

But Stamp-About was gone, and they heard him stamping down the garden path without his stick or his paper or his luggage. "*Pah*!" they heard him say. "*Pah*! That's the last time *I* ever make New Year resolutions!"

Poor old Stamp-About! He didn't know that although they were so very easy to make they're always hard to keep. *I've* found that out already, haven't you?